OFF LIMITS LOVER

Practice nurse Anya Fraser's adopted son is the centre of her busy life. But once her village clinic's handsome new senior partner Dr. Max Calder arrives, he is suddenly in her thoughts more than she's ready to admit. When extreme sports fan Max volunteers to help her with a terrifying charity parachute jump, they grow close. But Anya soon learns that the leap of faith she must take will impact on the home life she's fought so hard to secure.

JUDY JARVIE

OFF LIMITS LOVER

Complete and Unabridged

LINFORD
Leicester

First published in Great Britain in 2007

First Linford Edition
published 2017

*A catalogue record for this book is available
from the British Library.*

ISBN 978–1–4448–3506–9

Published by
F. A. Thorpe (Publishing)
Anstey, Leicestershire

Set by Words & Graphics Ltd.
Anstey, Leicestershire
Printed and bound in Great Britain by
T. J. International Ltd., Padstow, Cornwall

This book is printed on acid-free paper

1

Anya Fraser picked up the magazine and shuddered at the parachute jump picture. It looked exhilarating — *kind of* — but a part of her suspected it was a terror hell in freefall form.

The girl in the photograph sported vast orange aviator overalls that billowed in the wind. Hardly a look her wardrobe had been waiting to emulate. And g-force cheeks weren't something she was too keen to experience first-hand, either.

'That could be you,' came Katie's voice on the other end of the line. 'Wind hurtling past your ears, adrenaline pumping through your veins like you're powered by pistons. And a rugged instructor holding you close. Now that's what I call exciting. We could christen you The Parachuting Practice Nurse!'

Anya gulped.

That was what she called a personal Room 101.

More like her breakfast whooshing through her system to make a prompt reappearance in mid-air. *No thanks.*

The wild-haired female extreme sports enthusiast grinned out of the picture, arms across her chest in frenzied descent. Her parachute was firmly fixed to her back, her goggles framing a smile more like a grimace.

'How many miles up did you say it would be?'

'Ten thousand feet. In tandem with an instructor if you need extra support.'

Could there be enough chocolate in the world to persuade her stomach it could withstand a charity parachute jump? Anya doubted it. She pushed the magazine aside.

'I'll think it over. I wish you all the best with your efforts, but . . . '

'I'll work on you, you can't decline yet. We'll raise lots of cash. You can get the staff at the practice on board — a team of us, all securing much-needed money for Adoption Support. Maybe we'll fund an extra social work post? And we'll get press coverage. The support of your practice would be immeasurably valuable.'

There it was — Katie's clever persuasive ploy. And that was what made her so good at her job as coordinator for the East Scotland Adoption Support charity. The parachute jump would make a big difference. Plus, East Scotland Adoption Support held a special place in Anya's heart. It had helped her through the early days, after the placement of her own adopted son Callum. The boy who'd made her infertility and lost relationship battles bearable — her own little slice of golden-haired treasure.

'How can I say no?'

'Exactly. Too many good reasons to participate.'

More to the point, how could a woman with her 'heights aversion' realistically say yes?

'It's a bit more life-threatening than selling charity Christmas cards,' Anya pointed out wryly. 'Couldn't I cheer instead — like a mascot? With pompoms?'

'But think of the thrills. Callum will be so proud of his brave, adventurous mummy. He'll think you're epic.'

'Can't he settle for a mum who cooks a mean lasagne?'

Anya watched butter ooze down the holes in her crumpet. Suddenly, she couldn't face food, and pushed it away. The very thought of that freefall jump had turned her stomach queasy. Even if it did convince her son she was a superhero mum.

Why did Katie always insist on making her do these challenging things? Like confronting Grant about the separation, going through with the split after eight years together. Like completing the adoption process as a single woman. Like going out again — having a social life after Grant. Like taking control of her life again.

4

Anya balanced the cordless phone on her shoulder; it fitted snugly into the ample collar of her furry robe. She picked up her coffee and sipped. 'Did you say the instructor might be amazingly attractive? Great pecs, firm shoulders, a drool-worthy behind?'

Katie laughed. 'I'm a fundraiser. Not a miracle worker.'

Catching sight of her haphazard reflection in the glass door, Anya groaned. Sleepy blue-grey eyes looked back at her, complete with matching luggage. Her hair still had shower-wet stripes.

'C'mon, do something daring. Rise to the challenge.' Katie hammered her point home like an enthusiastic woodpecker. 'I know you'll succeed. It's there, shining bright, and you're evading the call to action.'

'Nope. I'm avoiding physical injury from plummeting from a massive height.'

During Anya's brief absence from

the lounge, the squirrel outside had reappeared. He habitually frequented her window ledge to perform death-defying tricks. He regarded her; perhaps he'd come to make her feel guilty about the jump? She normally encouraged him because Callum loved his cheeky antics, but today her sense of charity wasn't at home to visitors. And watching said squirrel leaping around in mid-air felt a little too close to their current topic for comfort.

'Have you heard the news about Dr. Calder?'

'No. What about him?'

Max Calder was a GP at the other practice in the small Scottish coastal village of Alderwick Loch. He had single women swooning, and the rest of the female population adoring his bedside manner and magical smile. He was dashing, mid-thirties, single, and as a joke among her friends it had long been quoted that Anya had once admitted to the attractions of the dark-haired, swarthy Scots doctor.

They'd dated during their schooldays too many years before, and recollections of his charms lingered even though the youthful pairing hadn't lasted.

In fact, Anya had once had a pure fantasy dream about him in full-kilted *Braveheart* guise. Heart-stopping stuff.

The grapevine suggested Max played the part of hero admirably too. He'd worked in disaster zones and done a stint as a voluntary doctor in Africa during his twenties.

'He's joining Cala Muir Medical Centre as senior partner. He'll be your new colleague soon enough. Apparently the announcement's due tomorrow. But Max told Belinda, who told me. The daredevil dreamboat doctor's going to be working with you. How's that for excitement?'

Suddenly, Anya wished she hadn't uttered that confession.

Drat, the perils of strong wine and friends with long memories.

Being a practice nurse in close proximity to Max. Wow, that would take some getting used to.

Anya parried with a noncommittal reply. 'I wonder why he wants to change practices?'

'Fresh challenge? The sexiest nurse in Alderwick Loch? How will you resist him — handcuffs?'

Anya burst into laughter. 'If you could see me now in my dressing gown, you so wouldn't be saying that.'

'Come on, Anya. Please say yes to the charity jump. I'll hold your hand going down if it helps.'

A wicked voice in Anya's head wished Max Calder were the instructor, and that *he'd* hold her hand throughout the ordeal. *Naughty wicked voice — back into a dark corner you go.*

A burning ember of anticipation caught light, shining enticingly, and Anya smiled into the phone.

Could she launch herself from a plane and raise funds from being foolhardy enough to try? If a man like

Max Calder could decide to swap jobs for a new challenge, surely she could face her silly fears and prove she had chutzpah enough to do this for her son. Could she counter the head demons that told her not to dare?

'Send me the sponsor forms and I'll give you an answer by Friday. But you owe me for this one.'

'How about a meal at San Remo tomorrow night? Pasta, fine wine, and a choc gelato dessert to tip the balance towards hedonism.'

'Done.'

'And you can tell me more about your feelings for the gorgeous Max Calder.'

'Some things,' Anya said simply, 'are going too far.'

Just then the front door flew open with a crash-thud against the wall.

'Callum, careful!'

'Mummy! I missed you!' Callum shouted from the doorway, where he was disposing of his jacket both arms at once.

'I'll have to go. That's Cal back from the childminder.'

'Keep reading that jump article in the magazine,' Katie instructed. 'It's our year for challenging new dares; we're running the risk.'

Anya's son Callum ran like a rugby tackler and made a head-butt dive right at her abdomen. She struggled for balance, and to replace the phone after saying farewell to Katie. He looked up at her grinning, his blonde hair fuzzy like an angel halo. Anya reflected that the winded feeling from Callum's buffeting would be similar to the breathless sensation of parachute jumping.

'Wait 'til you see the picture I've made you. It's of Martians invading from space.'

Right now, Martians were preferable to freefalling from aircraft for fun. Some things took time to work up sufficient courage to face.

★   ★   ★

10

'Max, come through, meet the staff!'

Retiring partner Struan McKendrick welcomed Max Calder into the throng, and urged him into the lemon-and-cream-decorated staffroom for his first team meeting. He wouldn't officially start for another week, but he'd agreed to come in today for the Cala Muir announcement.

'Thanks, Struan.'

Struan had promised they wouldn't bite. Yet there was one woman Max wished would nibble. Even if only just a bit.

Whenever he saw her around the village, Anya Fraser's big, blue-grey, dark-lashed eyes never held his for longer than two seconds maximum. Like she felt petrified whenever she saw him. Or she'd heard bad rumours. Or she didn't trust him. Or she hated men who sometimes went to football matches sporting designer stubble.

He'd counted the seconds, in fact. Two seconds — then those blue-greys skirted away from his.

'Hi — great football. Does Callum want to sit on my shoulders?' he'd offered once, ten minutes into the game of St Alders Athletic versus Cranntherston.

She'd declined fast. Nice smile. But still a put-down. He figured their brief relationship in their youth hadn't been as good an experience for her as it had for him. Which was more than a shame.

Nowadays, Anya often came down to St Alders with her son. He'd tried to chat. Too often she found some reason to extricate herself. He put it down to the fact that they'd dated in their younger years.

Max hoped their working relationship could transcend her apparent discomfort when he was around. Her mistrust. Her two-second eye contact limit. He secretly relished watching her, but guessed he was straying to places a doctor shouldn't go about prospective staff.

Max cleared his throat. The Cala Muir medical staff team smiled in welcome. Max smiled back.

Then he noted Anya's absence, and something tweaked at his subconscious to ask: *Why?*

A few seconds later the woman herself rushed into the room, looking annoyed at her late entry. He noted her breathlessness and the dark blonde strands of hair that tangled with her scarf.

'Sorry I'm late, everyone,' she muttered in apology. 'I had a seminar, plus the traffic's a nightmare. I had an unexpected patient to deal with.'

Hurriedly, she traversed the line of chairs to find her favoured position.

'Hi there, Anya,' he said casually. 'Glad you made it.'

'You haven't missed anything yet,' added Struan helpfully. 'I'm about to introduce our new senior partner who starts with us a week on Monday. We're very excited to welcome Max Calder to the team. He'll be leaving Glenfields and starting here shortly.'

This news was met with a brief ripple

of approval. Anya's gaze flicked to his, and they exchanged hesitant smiles.

'Perhaps you'd like to say a few words, Max?'

Max didn't want his staff thinking him a stickler for old-school ways. And then for several uncomfortable moments he failed to find the right phrases because his head had vacated the discussion topic. It had gravitated back to the newly arrived nurse.

Max pulled himself back into the moment. He rubbed his hands together to summon some clarity.

'I'm delighted to be here. I see this as a fantastic opportunity — you've a wonderful set-up. The team is an exciting one. This is a task I aim to rise to. I hope I can do you proud.'

Struan made a short speech about the challenges ahead, and Max nodded throughout. At one point, he caught Anya's eye, and noted her unconscious habit of biting her lower lip.

Max Calder would be giving himself a disciplinarian talking-to this evening.

Lusting after prospective colleagues was strictly not on.

The team dispersed. Anya, in contrast, headed straight for Struan. 'Could you take a look at Mrs Wallace? She's in the waiting room now,' she asked, her hand on his arm.

'Max, can you spare a minute?' Struan enquired, beckoning him over. 'Fancy giving us your prognosis here? We have a patient in need. Tell us more, Anya.'

'Jessie Wallace. She's having a glass of water outside. Someone at her lunch club called and asked me to see her because of a dizzy spell. That's why I was late. I brought her along — her friends say she's been acting strangely. Confused and disoriented.'

Max nodded. 'Can we see her now?'

'Lucy's keeping an eye on her in reception. I wanted to give her some quiet time.'

'Good decision,' Struan agreed. 'Max, could you have a look at this patient? I know you're not officially here yet; but, since this is an introduction, it might be a good chance to meet a few regular faces.'

Max agreed readily. 'I know Jessie Wallace, she's Maggie Wallace's mother-in-law. From the farm at Wayside.'

All three walked into the waiting area where they found Mrs Wallace looking pale, drawn and hesitant. Earlier, she'd been wobbly, confused, and having muddled conversations. Lucy, the temporary receptionist, told them Mrs Wallace was still in a puzzled state.

Max internally computed the symptoms: he'd examine her, but he had a hunch to follow.

'Hello again, Mrs Wallace,' he said, smiling down at the woman reassuringly, 'I hope you don't mind me looking after you today. I'd like to check a few things; nothing for you to be concerned about. We'll take your blood pressure and then a urine sample. Struan's going to stay in on this consultation as he's your doctor. Are you happy to let me assist?'

Mrs Wallace nodded, and let Max help her along the corridor to Struan's consulting room with Anya following close behind.

'I'm fine, Doctor. Light-headed, a little dizzy. It'll pass, it usually does.' Mrs Wallace patted Max's hand as if she needed to reassure him.

'So this is a common thing? Have you talked to a doctor before about this? Anything else worrying you at the moment?'

'No, you busy doctors don't need to be bothered with an old woman having a few dizzy spells.'

'Let me be the judge of that,' Max said gently.

He took Mrs Wallace's blood pressure, then ushered her to the patient toilet with Anya's help to collect a urine sample.

When she returned, Max told her, 'I'm going to call Maggie and ask her to fetch you. Tomorrow I'll be back in touch.'

'No need, lad,' Mrs Wallace objected. 'I'm tired. I need rest, that's all. Nothing a good sleep won't put to rights.'

'I'd rather be on the safe side by checking things. It's what I'm paid to do.'

He found Anya in the corridor and told her about the light-headedness not being a one-off. 'Sometimes,' he reminded her, 'elderly patients, ladies especially, can be prone to urinary tract infections which may also cause confusion and dizziness. I see from her notes that Mrs Wallace regularly receives incontinence pads. That makes me suspect her weak bladder control may have triggered an infection.'

'That makes sense, given her history,' Anya agreed.

'She might have an upper urinary tract infection, in which case I may need to refer her on to hospital. First, a high fluid intake is essential. We can prescribe antibiotics when we get the results.'

Anya told Max she'd known Mrs Wallace a long time, and she'd always been a spry, active woman, so this was an uncharacteristic episode. 'Thanks for your help on this, Max. I'd been thinking about her symptoms right through the meeting. She was so reluctant to come in.'

'Thanks for your actions. It's my job to double-check just in case, and I'll be here on a permanent basis soon enough. Maybe we could grab lunch next week?' he chanced. 'You could tell me the ins and outs of Cala Muir life. Like, where to get the best jacket potato; things not to do if you don't want to be on someone's blacklist . . . '

'Why don't you call me? Let me know about Jessie Wallace?'

'I will,' he promised. 'Count on it, Anya.'

Retreating down the hallway to get his coat and depart Cala Muir, Max resisted the urge to grin.

She'd held his gaze for five whole seconds. Great blue-grey eyes that pierced his soul and heated his thoughts.

Now, that was a Calder personal best.

2

'He asked you out to lunch?' Kate squealed, half-choking on her large glass of wine spritzer.

Anya looked pointedly at her. 'He's being friendly. It's an icebreaker, that's all.'

'Hey, don't try and wriggle out of it. I remember you told me that you dated. And that he still turns your head.'

'That was years ago, and before he became a boss,' Anya downplayed.

'Even more opportunity to get to know each other. And proof positive of attraction if you ask me,' Katie parried.

She kept strictly to herself that she could barely watch Max Calder without her heartbeat revving up to triple turbo. He still affected her. He literally made her blush from the feet up, and flutter, and say such daft things she had opted to keep quiet around him instead.

He had the kind of shoulders sportsmen aspired to and a smile an angel might kill for — as work colleagues went, he was a nightmare scenario on great legs. Even the sight of his dark-hair-peppered arms in that pale lilac cotton shirt with upturned sleeves had her thinking non-work thoughts. Even during his consultation with Mrs Wallace. Thoughts that perplexed her significantly.

What was all that about?

Anya pushed the scary attraction away. These fantasies were for private consumption only. Max would soon be her colleague, and romantic entanglements weren't something to consider. She couldn't get serious with men since Callum's arrival in her life. She wouldn't deprive her young son of her focus. And the discoveries of her fertility challenges with Grant meant she ducked relationships. She particularly couldn't handle men with risky adventurous habits (been there, done that with Grant).

It was well known that Max liked to live life on the wild side. He had dangerous hobbies; occasionally taking sabbatical treks to remote medical hot spots. Not your average guy by any stretch. Definitely off-limits.

Being out for a meal tonight felt like a welcome change, Anya reflected, diverting her thoughts from Max Calder. Even though she always felt a small chink of guilt about leaving Callum. Her mum was babysitting, but she worried even when she knew she shouldn't. Callum was her precious child; he'd only come to her at the age of two. She still revelled in every developmental milestone. The bond that other maternal mothers took for granted had had to be skilfully worked at. He'd always be, to Anya, a more special child because she'd worked so hard to forge attachment in view of the missed baby days.

But Katie refused to budge from the riveting topic of Dr. Max Calder. 'Heck, he's gorgeous, don't you think?

A bit George Clooney around the edges.'

'He's senior partner. So no more gorgeous conjecture.'

Anya nibbled at the garlic dough balls and forked her mixed green salad. Then looked up — straight into the face of the man they'd been talking about. Off-duty Max, in casual clothes, and staring at her with the kind of gaze that made her insides overheat. Anya gulped and sipped her wine, then ventured a smile.

Max came to stand by the takeaway counter in a dark leather jacket that won plaudits for bad-boy styling. He threw her a brief nod before talking to the server.

She stuffed the pasta she'd been twirling on her fork into her mouth, chewed, then swallowed before she could gasp aloud.

Help! Have we been talking loudly? Has he heard?

'Don't look,' Anya said through a fixed grimace. 'It's Max, and he's watching.' Suddenly she wished she could hide behind a super-slim menu and a tall pepper grinder.

Like the exhibitionist non-carer that she was, Katie swivelled fully in her seat and munched on her rocket-and-chicken pizza. She spotted him, extended a hand to wave in an obvious fashion, and called over, 'Yoo-hoo! Max! Join us, won't you?'

'Katie! Do you really have to?' Anya hissed.

But the comment came too late, as Katie had already found him a chair to draw up to their table. And with a smile Max was approaching.

'Caught out ordering takeaways?' Katie probed.

'I'm on call. Late dinner. Couldn't face cooking. Lame excuse but true. In the face of a San Remo pizza takeaway menu I submit every time. That's what I get for pinning it to the fridge. Serves me right — no restraint whatsoever.'

He and Anya shared a simmering glance.

Was it meaningfully dealt? She barely knew her own name under that stare, let alone what red-hot looks meant.

Under his gaze and his steady smile, Anya felt obliged to smile again too.

His lip curled slightly in a look she'd observed on film stars. Successful, sexy ones that were known woman-magnets. And from the way nearby female diners were waving and greeting him, he lived up to the analogy.

'Why don't you have some dough balls while you wait? We've plenty to share. Anya regularly over-orders on the dough balls. It's what she does best. She can be a wicked temptress when it comes to indulgence.'

Anya felt a blush zip over her cheeks, but rallied to try and come up with a suitable comeback. She didn't want her new boss thinking her a shrinking violet who hid and clammed up.

'Had a good weekend? Besides being on call,' Anya hazarded.

'Tinkering with the bike, mostly. It's my prize possession. But I went paragliding last week, which was fun.' He shrugged his broad, rugged shoulders, which she could imagine were toned and well worked-out from stimulating outdoor pursuits. 'Though next weekend I'm taking a party parachuting in the West Highlands.'

Max grinned and happily helped himself to a garlicky dough ball. As he licked the oozing butter from his thumb, Anya almost lost her pasta-laden fork.

'Parachuting? What a coincidence,' Katie squawked, then her laughter tinkled. 'We've signed up for a charity jump for Adoption Support Scotland. Since you're a pro, you'll have to join us. Help us get sponsorship. We could do with expertise and an extra on board.'

Anya winced inwardly. She wondered why Katie never checked before she jumped in at the deep end. Katie was a great woman, the best of friends — but sometimes her gusto for friendship pushed her headlong into domineering everyone into nearly everything.

'Max might be too busy . . . ' Anya started to say, chasing her dough ball round the plate and resisting the urge to stuff it in her friend's mouth to stop her talking.

Maybe she wouldn't feel comfortable doing her parachute jump from hell in the presence of Max Calder, her new boss. Correction: her new boss with his chiselled profile and charismatic manner. Could she stand to have him witness her every flailing effort? She'd rather fail at it alone, unobserved. In a quivering heap at the back of the plane refusing to jump and left to her own whimpering devices.

'I'd love to; when's the jump planned for?' Max replied. His eyes positively glittered at the challenge. 'Very commendable, I'm impressed.'

'Seven weeks' time,' said Katie. 'The plan is to jump in tandem with instructors at Shoresden Airstrip.'

'Seven weeks. You'll be working hard on raising funds now, then.'

'We're on the case. Anya can hardly wait either; she's a skydive novice.'

Anya felt blushes hijack her complexion at that. She pulled a face. 'My nerves are already in tatters. Seven weeks of dread coming up. Watch my fingernails disappear as the weeks go by.'

His sparkling indigo-eyed gaze sought hers. His eyes were smiling at her rebuffs and blushes.

She felt him flick over her in lingering assessment, taking in her appearance. Her dressed-up hair and filigree earrings and chiffon top suddenly made her self-conscious. Tonight she'd made more of an effort than her usual 'casual mum' look.

'Don't be nervous. It's a piece of cake. You'll do it, I have every faith.' Max reached over and patted her arm; the spot seared. Or was that her imagination? 'Next time I'm at Cala Muir, drop me a note of the dates. I'd love to join you, it would be a blast.'

'That's a matter of opinion,' Anya replied, this time managing to hold his gaze for longer than normal. 'Personally I'm petrified at the very thought of hurtling through the air towards the ground. Call me crazy, but the fear of smashed anatomy makes me nervous.'

He smiled, the magic volts of it dazzling her. 'Trust one who knows. The idea is far worse than the reality. I'm into extreme sports. Parachuting, snowboarding. The odd bungee jump. The exhilaration is tremendous! It's why they call me 'the daredevil doctor'.'

He pulled a grimace to indicate his distaste at the nickname. 'It makes me sound like some action hero with my kid patients. Otherwise I hate it. But if kids are happier to take their medicine when it's being prescribed by a daredevil, that's worth the pain. I tell them I can parachute in and catch them if they don't follow orders.' He touched the side of his nose lightly.

Katie laughed. And Anya felt her heart zoom a notch closer to liking him.

She could well imagine her own son falling hook, line and sinker for that approach. Inside, her heart drummed a fast tempo at an unexpected flicker of attraction. Shame he was a work colleague. Equal shame that one word alone could turn her brain upside down.

Max Calder kitted out in parachute gear would be irresistible.

He added, 'I could volunteer to take one of you in a tandem jump? Maybe Anya, since you're a novice and so nervous.'

'That's inspired,' said Katie with the widest grin she'd boasted all night, knocking back the vino in celebration.

Anya wished she could rewind or run away to avoid developments.

'Four Seasons pizza with mozzarella salad for Dr. Calder,' the server's voice announced, and the waiter approached with boxes.

Max smiled. 'Dinner's ready. Thanks for the chat, ladies. And the invitation.'

Anya saw another woman watch him

intently. *Resist those charms*, she warned herself.

The sensible adopter couldn't risk dating guys who flung themselves out of planes. She couldn't risk guys, full stop. She needed stability, not impulsive urges. Callum didn't need men flitting through his life. He just needed vast quantities of love from a doting mum.

So she wouldn't be strapping herself bodily to a hot man and jumping out of a plane with him.

'See you soon,' they chimed, giving each other knowing glances.

'See you at work,' he replied, and walked away.

They watched through the window as Max jumped on the big, bad and noisy new motorbike parked outside the window, and sped off. Off to rid the world of disease, parachute nerves and pizza toppings!

'Now, that's what I call tasty,' Katie purred. 'Next stop, lavish indulgent dessert on me. *He's* put me in the mood for decadence.'

Unlike her extrovert friend, Anya didn't intend to let her inclinations overrule her better judgement at every opportunity.

⋆   ⋆   ⋆

She was, Max decided on the ride home, both a fantastic prospect of a woman and a scary proposition all rolled into one exciting package. Daunting, too. Even to a man with a healthy reserve of daring.

The parts of him that Anya Fraser affected were those close to his weakest spot. The places Max didn't often go. The bits he'd shaken off.

And those took him right back to his gritty past. The raggedy, troublesome kid he'd been; always in trouble, at odds with a birth family who barely acknowledged his existence. The havoc he'd waged against his world, school, the police. No one would have believed he would ever have amounted to much; certainly not a sober, qualified GP, or a pillar of the local Alderwick Loch community.

And yet here he was, with a house he'd refurbished himself, a flash motorbike, sports car and a regular supply of interested dates (much to his amazement). Especially as he didn't really try to attract them. So far, he'd never met a woman who'd made a dent in his desire to roam and pursue the calling of his reckless gene.

Max pulled his bike into the garage he'd converted from a barn building at the back of his cottage two years before. These days, Cara Cottage did feel like home.

Home. Another scary concept.

Once upon a time he hadn't known what it meant other than beatings, arguments, disregard, cuffs to the ear, and maybe even the odd cigarette burn — or worse. Oh yes, he'd known the rough end of physical abuse.

Anya made him reflect on such things: the things he'd seen as a boy, and the scars that still ran deep.

Because Anya had an adopted son. She'd been through the arduous assessment process as a single woman. How much guts did that take? And commitment?

Parenting was hard enough, Max figured. But to struggle through the approval hoops of adoption and to go through the uphill struggle of the 'settling in' period of child placement without a partner for support — well, the only word that sprang to mind was *Amazing*.

How admirable was this quiet, unassuming nurse with the killer smile and watchable walk?

Anya's compassion reminded him of a woman very close to his heart; the special aunt who'd adopted him.

Could Max risk opening the trapdoor to his past? And could he keep such complex feelings separate from work?

He unclipped the pizza box from his bike and pulled off his helmet before locking the garage and heading indoors to eat.

Volunteering to parachute jump had been too good a gift. A chance to bond and show his commitment to the new job. Plus a chance to peel away the efficient, capable practice nurse veneer and investigate the enigma beneath: single adopter, side-line covert football fan, red-hot babe.

Max kicked off his boots, shrugged off his leather jacket, slid his pizza onto a plate and forked the salad straight from the plastic tub. He munched even before he found the comfy spot on the sofa and flicked the remote.

Then he reconsidered, picked up the phone and dialled, checking his watch. Aunt V should still be awake. But the phone rang three times before she answered.

'Aunt Violet? It's Max.'

Her familiar voice greeted him like a warm blanket. Especially when he heard the smiled joy from his pseudo-adoptive mother (from the age of ten when social services finally removed him from the family home from hell).

Aunt Violet would forever have a special place in his heart — so he should call her more. Not just when feeling the sharp stab of guilt.

'How's my favourite man? Still breaking hearts and saving lives?' Aunt Violet said, chuckling. 'When are you planning to visit me? That bramble jam's waiting in the larder, and I can bake your favourite scones at a moment's notice.'

Max grinned as he tried to swallow his San Remo pizza quietly so she wouldn't condemn his diet. He hid the emotion that was building in his chest and throat. 'Soon, Aunt Vi. How about this weekend? I could detour and drop by after parachuting's done? You can start baking scones for me tomorrow.'

'And when are you going to tell me you've found yourself a nice young woman to keep you at your own hearthside? When will the intrepid adventurer settle?'

'I guess when I meet her. And in the meantime, outdoor challenges keep me occupied and out of trouble. Now, those scones . . . How about Saturday?'

'When could I ever say no to you, lad?'

'It's a date, then. See, some women *can* tempt me to their hearths — and you're top of the list.'

* * *

For Anya, working as a part-time practice nurse was ideal for her situation. It was challenging work, but with flexibility sufficient to her needs and those of her son. She could play a valued role in her community, helping others, but her hours had been tailored to her number one, Callum.

Since Cal's arrival, she was no longer in a position to remain working full-time. As Anya viewed things, where would be the point in taking on the responsibility of a young child who'd been moved around during his short life, proving she was equipped for his needs, and then leaving him for the nine-to-five? She couldn't do it without feeling he was being cheated, so she'd gone part-time.

Anya's struggle to complete the adoption process after she and Grant decided to split had been a tough one. The process had been rigorous, perhaps even more so because of her single status. She'd had to repeat much of the adoption fact-finding exercise again solo.

It hadn't been easy, but the rewards were thousand-fold. Callum was her special little boy. He always would be. Lovingly, she studied his framed photograph on her desk. Maybe things hadn't exactly turned out like she planned, but still, she was blessed to have this young boy sharing her life.

Anya rose to welcome in her next patient. 'Come in, Jenny. How are you?'

Jenny Murdoch took a seat and smiled knowingly at the photo Anya had been looking at.

'Growing fast, isn't he?' Jenny exclaimed.

'Eats and eats,' Anya said wryly.

Sometimes it was hard to believe that Callum had once suffered plummeting weight from neglect, his basic needs ignored.

'And what a bonny boy he is. He'll break some hearts!'

'My mother's already.' Anya laughed. 'She spoils him silly. Now, what can I do for you today?'

Jenny took a deep breath. 'We've been trying for a baby for almost a year. I know it's early days, Anya, but I've been buying ovulation prediction kits from the chemist, and making sure my diet is ultra-healthy. I'm so very keen to start a family.'

Anya smiled. 'Those kits are expensive. And trying without success does take its toll. Why not rely on instinct for a bit? Give yourself a holiday? Enjoy your relationship and the bedroom side of things for its own sake.'

She recalled those feelings. The 'getting pregnant' obsession. Desperation for a tiny life to grow inside her womb, that yearning to be a mother.

She too had wanted it so very much, with all her heart.

In the end, it hadn't worked in her favour. But that didn't mean it wouldn't for Jenny — she was young, only in her early twenties. There was still plenty of time. Many healthy couples took a few years to conceive. Fertility wasn't an on/off switch, after all.

Jenny shrugged. 'I've even been taking my basal body temperatures each morning to gauge the fertile time, but it seems to be taking so long. My periods are like clockwork; I get so disappointed when they arrive. Sorry, I can't help the impatience. It's excitement, I suppose. We badly want to start a family.'

Anya nodded. She could remember being in that same position, taking her temperature to see the dip prior to release of an egg, then the later shift that indicated ovulation had taken place. She'd charted herself, but there had never been a pregnancy as reward. In the end, she'd stopped the rigorousness; it had been her attempt to control the situation, but sometimes you just had to accept a lack of control and be kind to yourself.

The desire for impending motherhood could become such a pressure in its own right.

'Are you taking folic acid supplements as we discussed last time?' she asked kindly. 'Still eating healthily, cutting out alcohol? I remember you're a non-smoker, which is good. That will help. Has Mike stopped smoking yet?'

Jenny nodded. 'And I'm eating loads of leafy greens and veg. In fact, Mike keeps joking I should get shares in the local greengrocer's.'

Anya smiled. 'You're both making a sterling effort. Only don't forget to relax. You're doing the right things. Still jogging, too. I haven't seen you pass my cottage window as often as I used to, but then perhaps that's because Callum keeps me so busy.'

'We both run. Though maybe not

quite as much now that we're concentrating on . . . on the bedroom.' Jenny blushed bright red. 'It feels strange, being so open about these things.'

Anya gently rubbed Jenny's hand. 'The most important advice I can give you? Relax, and try not to think about timescales. It only takes one successful time to make a baby. You're both young and healthy. Your menstrual cycle is regular. There are tests we can do later down the line, but they aren't necessary yet. Be patient and keep upbeat, enjoy being a couple for now. Have a few weekends away while you can. Take my word for it, when a baby comes, you'll wish you could do it over again.'

Jenny grinned. 'It's good to speak frankly.'

'You can come and ask me anything you like,' Anya reminded her. 'And relax, OK?'

Hiding concerns away and hurting was only a recipe for bitterness. Patients at her practice knew of her own struggles to conceive naturally. She'd gone through so many tests. They knew of her and Grant's devastation and IVF attempts. Then the relationship counselling, and the final trials of their partnership falling apart. But now at least she had Callum, and she'd wholeheartedly accepted her lot. What else could she have done?

'I will! And maybe I'll spend a little more time romancing Mike . . . '

Anya laughed. 'Enjoy your time together; baby-making needn't be boot camp.'

She closed the door softly behind Jenny, hoping that their efforts would yield that precious, longed-for gift of life.

The phone rang moments later and drew Anya back to her desk. The smooth, deep voice on the other end of the line caused her pulse to race immediately. It was her new boss.

3

'How are you today?' Max's voice down the line made Anya's pulse jive wildly. His tone was deliciousness with a hint of enigma thrown in.

'Oh, hi.' Anya feigned breeziness and watched her pen roll swiftly off her desk.

'So how are you? Busy? What've you been up to?'

Her brain inexplicably sprinted to wondering where Max was and what he was wearing. She marshalled her attention back into line.

'No, not too busy. I'm reading the new pamphlets about diabetes advice. Updating patient records and getting up to date on guidance notes. Basically sorting out my mess of an office desk.'

Gosh, she shouldn't have said that. Now he'd think she was a timewaster, filing her nails with her feet up, and he'd be investigating her workload first chance he got when he joined Cala Muir proper.

'What can I do for you, Max?'

'It's about Mrs Wallace. It seems she wasn't telling us everything about her state of health.'

'Oh?'

'As suspected, she's been concealing a urinary tract infection. It's been a contributing factor to the dizziness and confusion episodes. Mrs Wallace must have been in pain for some time. She's now admitted her incontinence has worsened, and she didn't want to worry her family. Apparently, she finds it hard to talk about these things, so you did well bringing her in. Goodness knows when she'd have admitted the truth on her own. She's now been informally chastised.'

Anya was amazed to think that poor Mrs Wallace had been bearing this alone and trying to cover up.

'Thanks for letting me know. Is she home now?'

'Resting. Under the watchful gaze of her daughter-in-law, who's determined to see a full recovery and insists she doesn't do too much. Anyway, I was meaning to ask . . . '

Anya panicked. She could feel a lunch date request coming. Without engaging her brain, she butted in. 'How was your pizza?'

Max paused, and chuckled lightly. 'Delicious as ever. Though I may start to put on weight soon because of my frequent custom there.'

It was her turn to laugh.

'I wanted to say I won't be available for a few weeks for the parachute induction,' he continued, 'but I won't forget. I'll still participate.'

'Oh, that's OK.' Anya was secretly pleased she wouldn't have to face her mid-air nemesis any time soon, yet strangely disappointed too.

'My next few weekends are all booked up. But maybe we could make some other arrangement?'

'Don't worry about it.'

'I'd like to do lunch though,' he added. 'Can you manage tomorrow?'

'Sorry, I can't make it,' she declined swiftly. It was neither a lie nor an excuse. She'd agreed to be a volunteer at an adoption training event, and was scheduled to talk to a group of new adopters. 'It's a shame, but I've got a prior commitment.'

'In that case, I don't suppose you're going to see the football at Alderwick on Saturday?'

'Actually, I am.' It would be senseless to lie; she already had her tickets, and she'd promised Callum.

'Then do you want to meet there? Maybe I'll treat you to a coffee and a doughnut.' He laughed. 'Can you tell I'm a pull-all-the-stops-out, high-life kinda guy?'

'That must be why you have such a fan club in the village.'

'Can I help it if I'm exciting?'

She recalled the sight of him on that dangerous motorbike. Straddling the engine as he pulled on his helmet. Or in that lilac shirt — smart, professional and in control. Jeepers! Working with this man was going to be pulse-racing stuff.

She counted to three, then went for it. A bit like her plan for the parachute jump when it came to taking the plunge.

'Doughnuts are dangerous.' She deadpanned for fun. 'My son may haunt you at every match from now on. Can you really risk that?'

'I told you, I'm into danger,' he said. Provocative to the hilt. He laughed then, and Anya found she loved it when Max Calder laughed back down the phone. 'Then it's a deal? I'll see you Saturday. I'll be the guy heading your way with the big fat box from Dan's Doughnut Van. Tell your son to come hungry!'

She smiled at the mental image, and hoped he'd sport the leather jacket again.

'That would be nice, Max, thanks.'

He hung up, still laughing.

A 'not date' with doughnuts and the daredevil doctor. Was she kidding herself by pretending she didn't like him? It was a tough call. Especially when her heart was pushing insistently, whispering. *Go on, it's just watching a football game from the sidelines with a four-year-old as chaperone. What harm can it do?*

'Why did you have to say yes?' she whispered to the empty phone line.

★   ★   ★

On Friday afternoon, Anya's day was cheered by the arrival of Gemma Stuart and her charming daughter Isla — one of Callum's nursery school friends.

'How are you?' she asked her young charge, who wandered into her consulting room in vivid pink dungarees and a matching stripy T-shirt, looking for the toy box she knew Anya kept for her smallest visitors.

'Fine. Callum and I made a great big sandcastle in the sand pit today,' said

Isla. 'He's very good at castles.'

'We've had lots of practice on the beach.' Anya nodded in welcome to Isla's mother. 'Her language skills are excellent now, Gemma.'

Anya was always keen to accentuate the positives, especially when dealing with patients with long-standing conditions. There was, after all, nothing worse than being faced with a lengthy negative list when you were patently aware of it yourself.

Isla had suffered from acute atopic eczema since ten months of age. Over time it had worsened, and the Stuart household had suffered substantial strain.

Isla had already undergone comprehensive allergy testing. Her nut allergy meant she'd had to be issued with an Epipen, an auto-injector for anaphylaxis. Isla's allergies could cause such an extreme reaction that the Epipen had to be kept with her at all times.

Past tests had identified that Isla was intolerant of dairy products, wheat, nuts and fructose. It had been a substantial weight for the family to bear, but they'd made a splendid effort in controlling her diet, experimenting and finding substitutes to appeal to a finicky four-year-old.

'How's it going? Are you coping?' she asked Gemma sympathetically.

'We've had a tough couple of months. Whenever she makes a big improvement, she suddenly reacts badly, her face becomes swollen, and then she scratches and gets infected.'

Anya nodded. Isla's night-time scratching did nothing to improve her facial eczema.

'How are the mittens?'

Isla's face turned to a scowl. 'I don't like them. Mummy makes me wear them.'

Gemma corrected, 'She takes them off. Repeatedly.'

Anya opened her mouth in faux shock. 'But those magic mittens are special, Isla. It's only very special people who get to wear them. Their magic dust brings fairies to visit the bottom of your garden, but it won't work if your mittens aren't on at night. Don't you want fairies to visit you?'

The small girl's face became a picture of awe. Isla looked between them, gaping; then seemed chastened and regretful. 'Would they really come? Maybe I could try again?'

'I'm sure the fairies will give you a second chance. Why not try tonight and find out? They don't want you to scratch and hurt your skin, Isla.' Anya winked at Isla's mum.

Isla nodded earnestly. Behind her, Gemma grinned and mouthed a heartfelt thank you.

'How's the new wet bandage-dressing routine?'

'The bandage body suits are excellent. And lightweight, so she doesn't get too hot. We're giving her stickers for telling us whenever she's hot. It avoids flare-ups, and rewards her for thinking about how she's feeling rather than scratching on impulse.'

'Well done; you're doing so well. It can't be easy.' Anya patted Gemma's arm.

Sometimes all the attention a sick child received could deflect from the remarkable work being done by the parent. And the significant pressure on the adult's life. Six months before, she'd referred Gemma to Struan, who had prescribed the girl's mother antidepressants. Caring for a child with these kind of demands had a definite negative impact. It seemed, however, that this had been turned around now.

'I'm coping. Taking each day and week as it comes. Not blaming myself or feeling a failure. I was caught up in a negative cycle before. I felt powerless to help her.'

From her own infertility experiences, Anya knew these were the kind of feelings that often triggered depression. In Anya's case, she'd opted for private counselling, a step she saw as a positive, proactive approach in moving forward.

'Good for you,' she told Gemma

encouragingly. 'And I'm here for you, anytime. You're tending a child with substantial needs, so make sure you schedule breaks for yourself.'

'I am. In fact, I wanted to invite you round to dinner with me and Sean next week. Sean will be cooking.'

Sean was a hotel chef, and his food was a gastronomic feast of mouth-watering local produce, seafood his speciality.

'Thanks, count me in.'

'Great. I've invited Max Calder too. I met him earlier in the High Street.'

Anya smiled; she could hardly take back her acceptance now, but it smacked of a trap. Even if it was kindly meant. So she issued a faux-stern warning. 'Two promises. No match-making, and ask Sean to do his signature chocolate mousse?'

Gemma extended a hand. 'That I can do. Come on, Isla, we've got to stock up on your reward stickers.'

Isla ran like a rocket to the door. 'Tell Callum to make me another giant sandcastle soon.'

'I will,' Anya replied, laughing to think that not only did she have an unexpected assignation to deal with, but so did her son. Only his would be confined to the sandpit.

Whose would be more fun, though?

★   ★   ★

'Mummy?' Callum sat up in bed and looked at her with serious eyes. Anya paused at the point she was at in the story book, which was about a crazy witch with purple hair.

She smiled. 'Yes, darling?'

'Why don't I have a daddy like Isla's?' he asked her, getting straight to the point.

Anya paused and internally took a deep breath. She could do this, no problem. She'd had the training, done the preparation work. One, two, three — stay calm and just answer his question.

'Mummy isn't married, honey. That's

why you don't have a daddy who lives with us. But you do have a birth daddy. He lives with your tummy mummy, Christina. They send you letters, and we send them letters and pictures back.'

She'd expected such off-the-cuff discussions to occur at some point. Just not this particular minute, blowing in like a whirlwind and making her edgy because her son was watching so intently. Ten minutes before lights out, and insufficient prep time for a considered Perfect Mum pearl of wisdom. Anya rallied as best she could.

'We've looked at the photographs, haven't we? Tummy Mummy Christina and Daddy Joe. You remember how we've talked about them? Not all tummy mums and dads can look after all their children. And that's why you came to live here, and I'm your always and forever mummy.'

Callum's gaze wandered as he absorbed her words. Then his brow furrowed.

'Nope, I don't mean them. I mean an

always daddy, like Isla has. He takes her to the park and plays football, and they go swimming, and he even fixes her bike. Sometimes he blows bubbles in the garden with a special bubble maker. Can't we have a daddy like that who'll help me fix my bike?'

Anya marvelled at just how much he'd thought this one through. Even at four, he was getting the hang of his peer network fantastically well, proving highly competent in sniffing out the daddy vacancy in the household.

'Mummy doesn't have a husband, sweetie. But I can fix your bike. Or, if I get stuck, we can ask Mr Steel at the bike shop.'

'Shame,' said Callum, looking super-cute in his Tornado Pete action hero pyjamas. 'I like Isla's daddy.'

'And you must remember that Tummy Mum Christina and Dad Joe love you very much. You're a very special little boy to have so many people who care for you.'

'I know.'

'That's good. Shall we finish the story now?'

An image of Callum on Max Calder's shoulders — giggling at being thrown around by strong arms — popped inexplicably into her brain to replay in soft focus.

Anya tried to shake the thought away. But even though she evaded the family snap in her head, she was still struck by how handsome Max looked as a pseudo-dad. And how happy Callum had appeared with the daddy figure in her fantasy.

Anyway, Max is far from 'safe forever dad' material. Didn't I learn any lessons from Grant?

Max's need for thrills and adventure was probably in the blood, a genetic predisposition. Something that couldn't be sidelined or tucked away. And hadn't Grant paid dearly enough for his own inclinations in that department? Grant's rally compulsion had been something that had eventually pushed them apart and resulted in tragedy.

She told the rest of the story. But her mind was elsewhere the entire time. Callum's prior plight in the early days of his life still squeezed her heart. She had empathy for any parents losing a child, but her heart felt heavy for the children who suffered neglect.

Anya finished the purple-haired witch story, kissed her sleepy son goodnight, and stroked his downy soft head.

Before he finally dropped off to sleep, she lulled him with a story about a girl who took to the air to learn how to fly. The look on Callum's face at her description of whirling through the clouds on a parachute was priceless.

She watched him in peaceful slumber. He did seem to think she was a supermum — making all her lengthy legal battles for him worthwhile.

'I'll do it for you,' she whispered in the darkness. 'Jumping from a plane is no big deal when it's for you, darling.'

She treated herself to a glass of chardonnay from the bottle at the back of the fridge when she went downstairs, but only managed one sip before the phone rang.

'It's Katie. How's it going?'

Anya smiled. 'Fine,' she told her. 'Except that Callum's been asking why he doesn't have a daddy. Do you think he's missing a male role model?'

'It's all natural stuff, Anya. The boy's making strides towards exploring his world. And, speaking of male role models — how did lunch with Max go?'

She sighed at her friend's persistence. 'I couldn't make it, busy schedule.' She refrained from mentioning that they'd booked an informal tryst instead at Saturday's match.

Then Katie surprised her completely. 'My nephew Jamie's here on a visit; the one who's started in A&E. He fancies coming to tomorrow's game, and asked if he could tag along with Callum? Any chance?'

Typical, thought Anya drily. If she didn't say yes, Katie would suspect something. And if she told her friend about her arrangement to meet up with

Max tomorrow, she'd pry. But then, St Alders Athletic F.C. was hardly a dinner date in a cocktail dress. And Max Calder was a mature guy who'd understand her predicament. Anyway, it wasn't a date; and after Callum's questions that evening, she certainly didn't feel ready to start anything.

'Of course Jamie can stand beside us,' said Anya, taking another sip of her wine and enjoying the sharp but warming feeling inside. 'He'd better cheer on St Alders, though. Any defecting and he's toast, you tell him from me.'

'He'll be as keen a supporter as you wish. Come on the Loch Lads! Score and save the day.'

Anya replaced the phone as guilt tugged at her conscience. Would Max appreciate Jamie's presence? And, truth be told, would she?

4

As Anya dressed her son prior to the match, her heart danced with the kind of love that had resonance in her. Clad in a hat and scarf in the village team's red and white colours, with his apple cheeks and golden hair, Callum was as fine a sideline mascot as she'd ever seen. Even if, as his proud mum, she was utterly biased.

The weather was crisp and typically Scottish autumnal as they wandered down to the ground from her cottage in Whin Wynd. Usually she donned her pale green ski jacket and a hat. Today, she'd made a smidge more effort. She'd pulled on her grey tweedy coat — the one that brought out her eyes — and matched it with a downy-soft chunky scarf in duck-egg.

She even wore make-up and lip gloss. Luckily, Callum never noticed such

63

things, unless it was lipstick. He hated lipstick, and called it 'lip goo'.

At the ground she ran into Jamie, looking young and dashing, the image of the new A&E heart-throb who would have the young nurses flocking.

'Jamie, Jamie!' Callum shouted, hurling himself at the young man who'd previously captured his affection by spending an hour showing him penalty kicks in Katie's garden.

Jamie whirled the boy round and pulled him onto his back without ceremony. 'Want to ride on my back into the ground?'

Cal clamoured in ready agreement, but as Anya smiled, her tummy was jigging in anticipation. Max had told her he'd meet her inside.

Was he here?

She scanned the crowd without success, so followed Jamie inside. Alderwick's football ground wasn't exactly a prestigious stadium, but it still became crowded on a Saturday, pre-match. No doubt Max would find her soon enough, though.

'Mummy, hurry up, slowcoach!' shouted Callum as Jamie turned with her waving son on his back.

'Hold your horses!' Anya hoped she would manage to hold a cogent conversation with her new boss when he arrived.

* * *

Max saw her scanning the crowd, and started to walk eagerly forward to greet her. She looked amazing. So amazing it caught in his throat. Then he faltered.

Who was this young guy who'd stolen his thunder by scooping Callum onto a glory seat first?

Max was unsettled, especially when he felt a tiny curl of envy he didn't care to admit to. He rallied, and caught up with Anya and Callum — plus the unidentified man who was crashing his date — just as they were taking their seats near the away goal.

'Hi, Anya, Callum, how are you?'

Max bent forward to claim a surprise kiss on her cheek that he hadn't even planned to give her.

'Max, great to see you,' she replied. She suited the duck-egg colour of the scarf that framed her face so perfectly. He wished he had her all to himself.

'I'm Max,' he said, turning to the younger man, 'and you are?'

'This,' said Anya hurriedly, 'is Jamie McPherson. He works in A&E in Edinburgh. He's also Katie's much-loved nephew, and Callum and he are thick as thieves. I promised they could team up at football.'

Max's brain admitted that his jealousy was a case of 'doctor in the wrong'.

'Good to meet you, Jamie.' Max grasped his hand in a gauntlet-type shake, then cajoled his mouth into a smile. 'You like Alderwick?'

'I like all football. And I promised Callum I'd tag along next time I was visiting my aunt.' Jamie ruffled Callum's hair.

'Good. I mean, great. Nice for Callum.'

Was it his imagination, or was his date looking at him strangely?

Max pulled up the edge of his leather jacket against the chills, trying to look cooler than he felt.

Chill out, he told himself, *you're blowing it.*

★ ★ ★

The football match passed quickly; which was good, Anya told herself, stamping boots against the terrace stand because of the chill air. Unfortunately Jamie's presence and Max's odd mood meant the 'non date' passed without as much conversation as she'd anticipated.

She did get a fab glimpse of Max up close. She enjoyed his mid-match banter abusing the 'sight-challenged' referee.

'I'll tell him you want him to get his sight checked,' she confided. 'He's a practice patient. Maybe he'll be on your list.'

His eyes met hers in stark shock before he burst into laughter. She found those eyes, now that she was letting herself look into Max Calder's eyes when he spoke to her, had her hooked. The darkest blue that spun her reason and left her powerless but to smile back, transfixed.

Then, ten seconds into extra time, it happened.

Stevie Nairn flew into a brave tackle intended to snatch a pristine chance at goal, but the wince-inducing thud of his opponent's boot had him floored and writhing in agony. Max patted Anya's shoulder to indicate a speedy departure was in order. He ran down to the sidelines to assist, jumping onto the pitch and into the thick of things like a seasoned pro sports medic without a second thought.

Minutes later, he was joined by the physio and medical staff. Stevie was stretchered and substituted, and Anya's date abandoned.

It was some consolation that Alderwick won three-nil, but not much for Stevie. Max told her later by text from the hospital that the player had suffered severe damage to his knee ligaments. It would take recuperation and therapy before he'd play again.

'So much for the pre-match effort,' she told herself. 'He hadn't even got around to the promised box of doughnuts!'

Was a date with Max Calder always so promise-filled, and yet ultimately disappointing?

★   ★   ★

At quarter to ten Anya gave herself permission to pour a glass from the remains of the wine she'd started the night before. She was taking a tiny sip when she heard a soft knock at the front door.

To avoid waking Cal, who was fast asleep, she tiptoed to the door barefoot.

The unexpected visitor on the threshold still surprised her completely.

'Max, come in! How's the patient?'

'The surgery was successful. Though I know he'll be depressed for his career goals when it all sinks in. He had high hopes for this season. Sorry to pop by so late. I didn't want to wake Callum, so left my car at mine.'

'Come through.'

Why did he have to look like he'd just dropped in from some gathering of the Handsome Men Clan — all dark hair curling at the nape of his neck and big jacket muffling him as his breath came out in chilly clouds? In a word, delicious.

'I don't mean to disturb you. I didn't get a chance to speak properly after Stevie's leg.'

She beckoned him inside. 'No problem. Jamie walked us back.'

Max raised a brow but made no comment. 'Callum in bed?'

'Sound asleep. Thanks for not ringing the doorbell.'

Half of her itched to offer him the remaining glass of wine in her bottle so she could finish her own. The other half didn't trust herself with alcohol and Max Calder — alone and one-to-one.

'Tea or coffee?'

'I won't stay. I just wanted to say some things. Sorry the date was a washout.'

Date. He said 'date'.

Now he was messing with her mental goalposts. She took a breath, but all she succeeded in doing was breathing in his manly cologne. And the fresh woodsy smell was nice, very nice.

Anya nodded to the comfy jade green sofa that would have been tidy had it not been for Callum's action figures propped around its cushions as if on desert manoeuvres.

'Sit down, won't you?'

'Did he enjoy the game?' Max raised his eyebrows.

'Oh, yes. Especially the injuries. I fear he has either medical inclinations or gruesome curiosity,' Anya said. 'Listen

— about Jamie tagging along. I'm sorry if — '

Max interrupted her. 'No, it's me who was out of order. Me who should apologise. I figured Jamie was your boyfriend, and I won't deny that bothered me. Then I realised it served me right. We were just two friends meeting to watch football. I guess it made me admit it meant more to me than I'd let on.'

Anya couldn't help noticing his full lower lip. The wonderful texture of his skin. She longed to trace his jawline and see what that faint beard shadow felt like. But she bit back the inclination.

Instead, she leant forward on her knees and stoked the fire, belatedly realising it was a stupid idea because in doing so she was giving Max a full view of her backside in jeans . . . and they were tight, too! The ones she had a feeling should be left to svelte models, not post-thirty mothers who'd split them at the knee, rugby-scrumming with her son.

Anya Fraser, she chastised herself. *When are you ever going to learn some guile?*

★ ★ ★

Covertly, Max watched that shapely rear framed by a real log fire. The woman inside the jeans was as impressive as the view.

Now, *this* was the sort of quality time he'd envisaged in his fantasies.

How he wished he was familiar enough with Anya to tug her back by the belt loops for a fireside kiss. He itched to take her by surprise, and the thought lodged in his brain. She was his very own fallen piece of heaven. With a tantalising hint of sin thrown in.

'So, what can I help you with tonight, Max?'

He dragged his attention away from her assets and let his eye rove the room instead, taking in her colourful eclectic style. The cottage was cosy, neat but homely, with funky pictures and vivid scatter cushions in ginghams. Her style was more girly than he'd have suspected, but he liked it.

'I wanted to speak to you.'

He had ground to make up. Explanations to give. For being a jerk about Jamie, and for leaping over the football barrier to play sports doctor.

If she didn't think he'd been an idiot at the match, she ought to. Getting jealous and frustrated because she'd taken a chaperone for company had been an overreaction. And that annoyed him.

Max reached into his jacket pocket and drew out the envelope he'd put there earlier.

'This is a donation,' he said briskly. 'I'd like you to give it to Adoption Support Scotland on my behalf. I feel strongly about it being an exceptional cause, so I hope it helps in the fundraising. I know how hard you and Katie are working to raise money, and I want to give support.'

Anya had turned away from the fire

now and watched him, her expression incredulous. 'You don't have to do that.'

'I want to.'

Eyes met and lingered. Her gaze seemed to slide away, before slowly coming back to search his face.

She flicked open the envelope and glanced down at his donation, clearly surprised. 'This merits a glass of chilled wine! It's a very generous donation.'

He shrugged, itching to beckon her towards him and push the stray tendrils of honeyed hair away from her cheeks. 'It's something I feel passionate about. I'll explain later. Can I have that wine now?'

She smiled at him. 'I'll have a glass too. Katie will be over the moon about this.'

She disappeared into the kitchen and fetched them both chilled glasses of wine. Then she sat nearby and smiled at him invitingly. Had it not been for the discussion he so badly wanted to have with her, he might have taken the glass from her fingers and pulled her towards him.

Max shoved the inclination far away.

'I wanted to make this donation because it's for something that matters to me on a personal level. I appreciate the kinds of issues these kids have in their background. My aunt informally adopted me. She took me in at age ten, and stopped the spiral of bad behaviour, dire parenting, and me running away from home every month. So I know the chaos these kids come from, and how money can make a difference. There — I've said it.' He forced a wry smile. 'I was adopted. I was a bit of a tearaway. Not many people know that.'

She leant forward and touched his arm. 'Max, I don't know what to say.'

An electric charge he recognised as a mix of attraction and confusion zipped through him. Desire wasn't an appropriate response in this situation. Yet still he felt it.

'I was lucky, like your son. We escaped and got help. And for what it's worth, I think you're amazing — adopting as a single woman. That takes guts. Sometimes adopted kids come with baggage even they don't understand. They fight because they're angry inside, even the little ones. So you have my utmost respect.'

It would be so easy to say *Hug me*, he thought. *Kiss me, make it go away, hold me tight to allay the ghosts inside.* How he longed to brush his mouth over hers — seeking salvation in her sweetness.

It didn't feel great getting it off his chest, but he was relieved that he'd come clean. He'd told her — *almost* — why he felt they had such a special bond.

'I'm very glad you've confided in me, Max. I can see now why you want to give us this donation.'

Max shook his head, deciding to be completely honest with her. 'It's not just altruism. I'm also attracted to you. But I realise the last thing you need is a relationship at work. I want you to know, if you need a friend who understands, I'm here. And while I'd like there to be something between us, I won't push you.'

Max rose from his seat.

'You don't have to go,' she stammered. 'Stay, please.'

He sat back down, and she continued hurriedly, 'Max, I'm not as worthy as everyone seems to think. Adopting Callum was a personal decision. Grant's career aspirations had driven us apart. He'd outgrown Alderwick and he had no interest in adopting another family's child. Some people might think I was the selfish one, that I was the one who got what I wanted. But I couldn't compromise on having a family. That's why I don't go round looking for relationships.'

'You're not selfish,' he reassured her, 'you're pragmatic. You went for what you wanted, and risked losses along the way. In my book, that's immensely brave. Don't play it down.'

'I don't feel comfortable about relationships. They come with too many expectations. I don't ever want to go through all that again. This isn't a personal snub, Max.'

The way she looked at him when she said that made his throat tighten and his lips itch to kiss her. It almost made him jump, the desire to get closer to this woman was so intense.

'I respect that.'

She nodded, looking away. 'Thanks. When you can't have a child, people are either embarrassed, or they want to smother you with platitudes and act like you're saintly. Believe me, I'm far from saintly.'

Somehow, he wished she'd show him that side of herself. Right now.

'I'm a doctor, remember. Empathy is part of the job description. I'm here as a friend if you need it. Yes, I'd love to take you out. But I'm not foolish enough to think I can talk you round if you aren't ready.' He smiled. 'I guess I'm just registering my interest. Without any pressure.'

'Thanks for your honesty.'

Slowly, he put down his wine glass. 'To all intents and purposes, I was adopted by my aunt. Without her, I wouldn't be the man I am today. She made me realise my own worth. I'd probably be in prison now if it wasn't for her, my behaviour was so wild and reckless in those days. So I understand more than most.'

He got to his feet and zipped up his jacket. It was time to leave. He didn't want to push things tonight and wreck her trust. But he couldn't help one last attempt.

'Let me take you out to dinner,' he suggested. 'Not as a colleague, or as a guy with the hots for you. Though I guess both are true.' He grinned at her expression. 'Let's go out to eat and just hang out as friends.'

'A friendly pizza?'

'A friendly Mexican, Indian, Thai meal. Whatever, it's your call.'

'I love Thai,' she admitted. 'Maybe you're worth the risk. How are your table manners?'

'Try me.'

She raised her eyebrows, then lifted his heart inside his chest without even uttering a word. Her smile had the power to do that. It was, Max decided, a smile that he knew would haunt him for days, nights, maybe weeks to come. But he'd done what he came to do tonight.

'I'd like that very much, Max.'

Standing on the threshold, she sealed their meeting with a light kiss on his cheek, and he had to stifle a groan along with his surprise.

'You'd better be a nice boss or I'll change my mind.'

'Good behaviour. I've never tried that approach before.' But he was smiling as he retreated.

5

Anya dreamed of Max the next morning, in the pale hours where dawn meets the day.

In her fantasy, they were dancing for some unknown reason which could in no way, shape or form be connected to work. But the music was soft and slow, his hands on her lower back a warm comfort as they moved to the rhythmic jazz.

'I've wanted this for so long,' he confided to her softly in the dream.

'You're not the only one,' she murmured.

His strong athletic body had her pulse racing circuits, and his breath on her neck caused an inner meltdown.

She pushed her lips to his in smiling welcome. He smelled of citrus with an edge of something spicy that was addictive.

A loud alarm beep tore her fantasy down like a vandal tearing drapes from a window. Reality's daylight streamed onto the scene — and her subconscious was laid bare.

She turned her head and glanced at the digital alarm clock. Six-fifty-nine. Max was nothing but a dream.

For a woman who'd once claimed trying for a baby had caused her burnout, she was doing nicely in the interest department with the right dance partner. With Grant, it hadn't been about pleasure at the end. It had been about pain and despondency at their lost dreams. A mutual ache, both of them wanting a baby.

'Oh, heck!'

A working Monday stretched ahead. One in which she'd have to face the object of her fantasies at unexpected moments. No doubt looking handsome and professional, and making her blush at her own secret thoughts.

Max Calder was exactly the wrong kind of guy for her. She wasn't ready to go back to relationship territory either; she had Callum to consider now. She wouldn't be getting involved even if Max did inspire secret dreams. And danger in the extreme.

With a groan she leapt from bed and headed for the bathroom. Time for a shower, she told herself sternly, to restore her sanity.

* * *

The September sunshine made a last-ditch bid to pretend it was still summer instead of dawning autumn. Anya went to work all too aware that it was Max's first day at Cala Muir Medical Centre.

She walked Callum to nursery, and then continued on to work, rather than take the car. She wanted to savour the memories of walking on bright days to see her through the long dark winter ahead.

Only half an hour into her working day, the presence of the new senior partner was already tangible. Max was making an impact, in a good way. It seemed the staff were already highly impressed with him.

Lynette, the office manager, was singing Max's praises in the staffroom over coffee.

'He's so thoughtful,' she told Anya. 'And interested in my suggestions for improvements. He's got some ideas for us to run some training sessions for diabetes and asthma sufferers. Also some short courses in first aid.'

Even Anya was impressed at this snippet of news on his progressive ideas, but she kept her expression neutral, determined not to join his growing fan club.

Later, when she passed the health visitor, she heard Abi saying, 'Max wants to chat about my key concerns for developing the service. He's going to make a big difference here.'

She'd only been passing through the back office on her way to find some records. But that didn't stop her colleagues from trying to draw her into the Max Calder praise session.

She gave a noncommittal, 'He's certainly tuned in,' and dashed back to her office under the excuse of pressing work. Then she shook her head at herself.

Keeping a low profile and getting on with a normal day had seemed the best option. But was it so easy? Especially in view of her early-morning fantasies . . .

She blushed fierily. If any of her work team guessed what she was really thinking about the new team member, they'd have fuel for gossip for months.

She also found herself wondering, were all women so enamoured by Max 'Say the Right Thing' Calder?

Anya vowed to ensure she was so absorbed in her work, she wouldn't have an opportunity to see him. She'd be polite and courteous, but strive to avoid personal discussions.

That day, their contact was limited to a brief 'Good morning,' as he passed her in the corridor. Though that innocent enough greeting had been enough to kickstart her pulse. He'd smiled in passing, and she had found herself noting the dark spring of his hair, and how the pale aqua of his shirt suited his colouring.

Truth was, she regretted her lapse in kissing him on her cottage doorstep when they parted. Especially after his revelation that he felt there was chemistry between them, and he'd like for there to be more.

There were no half measures with Max. Chastened by her reaction to that 'Good morning,' she avoided him the rest of the day.

The next day dawned bright and clear. At ten-thirty, Anya received a welcome lunch invitation from Katie. Since Katie was great at doing home-made lunch spreads, it was too good an opportunity to miss. Escaping the office was an entirely desirable prospect too. Who could miss or avoid watching as he strode around on long, athletic legs? She had his cheque for Adoption

Support to deliver to Katie, so an escape was both prudent and necessary.

Only upon arrival at lunch did she start to rethink the decision. Katie sniffed out emotional undercurrents like a police dog on duty.

'Wow!' Katie looked up from the cheque, her face burning with curiosity. 'What did you have to do for this?'

'Nothing,' Anya replied blithely, ignoring her insinuations.

'Is he in love with you?' Katie studied the cheque in her hands. 'This is major. Either the man's in total lust or he's earning far too much money. This is fantastic.'

'Hold your horses!' Her face suddenly hot, Anya stalled Katie's thought-train. 'He's not doing this to curry favour with me. He has a lot of compassion for the charity, that's all.'

They were sitting at the big old pine table in Katie's kitchen, enjoying glorious views of the loch through the large windows. She'd prepared a spread of tuna-crunch thick hoagie bread rolls,

Earl Grey tea and home-made cookies. And as they munched and sipped, the fishing boats on the loch brought in their catches, looking as small as Callum's toy versions from that distance.

'Don't go adding two and two and coming up with ninety, Katie,' Anya admonished her friend.

'I'm just saying he's showing a lot of interest. Enough to deliver that cheque personally.'

'And now it's been safely delivered to you.' She focused on her delicious lunch and tried to remain unfazed by the interrogation. 'It would be churlish to tell the new senior partner to get lost. *Oh Max, can you make sure you stand at least thirty feet in the opposite direction from me in future at all football matches?* Hardly welcoming!'

'I have a hunch he's interested. Maybe he'll ask you out?'

'Enough, Katie. Change the topic.'

'But I'm just getting started. Jamie said you seemed a handsome pair and that you got on very well together.' Her friend smiled mischievously. 'How is Max fitting in at the surgery?'

'Great. But this is only his first week in the post.' Anya shook her head in exasperation. 'He's my boss,' she continued, 'and nothing's going to happen. I can't stay long, by the way. I have to get back for a patient soon.'

Katie fixed her with a hard stare. 'You wouldn't be the first colleagues in history to be sighing wistfully after each other. Enjoy the attention; grab some social life while you're at it. It could lead to more — you're both free agents.'

'And I've a four-year-old son, which makes me ineligible for the social circuit, Katie.'

'I'm available for babysitting. You're over thirty and it's legal. Plus, Max is gorgeous. What's to question? As for the cheque, we'll send him a formal thank-you note, but you can thank him profusely from me in the interim. I also meant to say, tomorrow we've got a photocall scheduled for the charity jump. The local rag wants a team shot. You, me, Max and Tina in parachute gear outside the surgery — to drum up local support.'

Anya found herself shying away from that idea. Publicity wasn't something she did. Callum's placement had anonymity issues attached. For, while she'd met both his birth parents several times, and they knew the general vicinity of their son's location, they had no specific address for Callum. They hadn't wanted to voluntarily give Cal up, but had been forced to legally. Contact with their birth son was out, due to his father's volatile temper. Could she risk a photo in the local paper?

'What about Callum? No names, remember?'

Katie nodded. She was well aware of the issues attached to Callum's case.

'Don't worry, it's only the *Craig Shiel Chronicle*. It'll be circulated around the local villages as far as Menteith, but no further. Besides, what's a little publicity when you're about to fall from a great height? You may as well inform the neighbourhood how nuts you are.' Katie smirked. 'Tell Max to be ready, would you? The photographer's coming tomorrow at noon.'

Anya picked up her jacket and bag. So much for the lunchtime escape route from Max Calder. It had felt like all they'd done was discuss him from start to end.

'I'll see you tomorrow,' she said lightly. 'And give up on the Max hassles, OK?'

★ ★ ★

Max strode through Cala Muir's reception the next day in pale khaki aviator overalls that should have carried a censorship warning. He was every woman's private *Top Gun* fantasy. Or Anya's, anyway. Even in unflattering utility wear, he made it a superhero look.

Was she losing her wits lately? All she seemed to have on the brain when it came to Max was heated thoughts. She recognised the now-familiar way her pulse throbbed when their gazes locked.

'Ready for adventure? Hey, where's your suit? Not turning chicken, are you?'

'I'm running late. Do we *have* to wear those?'

'Yes.' He smiled. 'No half measures when Katie's in charge.'

In spite of the comic overtones of his words, that hot look had told her she was *highly* susceptible to him. She'd have to work hard to keep him at arms' length if she was to stay level-headed about this crush.

'Here, put these on, get a move on,' Katie instructed, rushing past them a moment later and throwing her a set of overalls. A nightmarish memory of the parachute jump photograph from the magazine lurched into Anya's brain. Now that it was becoming real — this crazy idea about jumping from a plane

— she felt a sudden raw terror at the prospect.

'Oh dear! I'm sensing a fashion mistake at twelve o'clock.' Anya cringed. 'The jumpsuit look isn't a flattering one for me, I look like something from a cartoon.'

'Don't quibble. It's a photocall,' Katie parried. 'We have to enter into the spirit.'

Max's low voice sounded softly beside her. 'I'm sure you'll make it a hot look. Though my preference is for you relaxed and in jeans by firelight.' He was trying to stop the grin by biting the corner of his lip.

She shot him a warning glance, shocked at his blatant lack of guile.

Max stared back and his eyes flicked a quizzical entreaty.

'Don't go there, please! We're at work,' she whispered.

Was he baiting her, slipping back into the familiar way they'd talked in front of her fireside?

'Do you want us with or without

goggles?' Max checked, looking away first and breaking the spell. 'The goggled look might be better. So we can hide behind them.'

Katie smiled in an angelic fashion. 'Max, I don't mind what you choose. You're always handsome, whatever you wear. But why not put them on top of your head — best of both worlds?'

Anya threw Katie a chastening look which her friend ignored, smiling back at her with saccharine sweetness.

Anya said abruptly, 'I'll go and change, then; just give me a moment. Though we must be mad doing this.'

'We're being good sports,' Max told her, holding Anya's gaze steadily. 'Get the suit on and you'll feel differently, trust me.'

'Yes, if I can work out how to get into these things in the first place.' Anya tucked the pale khaki overalls under her arm and headed for the ladies' loos.

'If you need a hand, just call me.'

She turned at Max's shocking parting

shot and caught his gaze. His expression was of wry amusement.

It had, it seemed, only been a joke.

Yet why was he being so informal in his dealings? He should know better. Having the new senior partner say provocative things in public wasn't on. Especially when her own longings were on overdrive.

She threw Max a withering glance. 'I don't need your help, thanks. I'll meet you both outside.'

'I'm sorry,' he started to say, but she strode off without waiting to hear the rest of his apology.

Struggling into her parachute suit, Anya had ample time to regret snapping at him like that. His comment probably had been a joke, but it was too late now. She'd overreacted, and had just had her first unofficial run-in with the boss.

6

For the photocall, they had to pull some huge grins and do thumbs-up and classic happy poses, all of which left Anya feeling uncomfortable after her overreaction. But the reporter from the local paper was helpful and put them at their ease quickly. He promised to use the photo in colour to drum up financial support from local readership, and said that the picture was possible front-page material.

'Fame at last,' Katie cooed excitedly.

'Our madness trumpeted throughout the land in Technicolor,' Anya replied, and they all laughed.

For the final set of photographs, the four of them stood like some superhero quartet — arms braced across their chests, goggles in place and fixed smiles on their faces.

She was intensely aware of Max's

presence beside her, but managed to pull through unscathed. The jolt of awareness he gave her was daunting but she had resolved to ignore it.

He's your new senior partner. One of the team. Get over it!

She tried to control the twirling, excited knots in her stomach, the goosebumps his touch on her elbow had inspired. And she pretended he didn't look gorgeous in that khaki suit. He was a colleague, and not her ideal boyfriend choice.

As the photographer thanked them for their time, a blue estate car sped up outside Cala Muir's entrance, a screech of tyres underlining its haste.

'What's up?' Straightening up, Max nodded his head in the direction of the vehicle.

'No doubt we'll soon find out,' Anya murmured.

The driver hurried around and opened the door for his injured passenger.

'That's Eddie Carsdale from the

Bracken Café,' Anya said in surprise. 'It looks like he's been hurt.'

They sprinted over to the car to help Eddie and his daughter Rhona into the surgery. The driver was William Mays, a one-time Alderwick resident who'd been working overseas for over a year. At one time William had shown some romantic interest in her, in the midst of Callum's adoption application, and she'd had to turn him down. He looked across at her, but Anya's instincts kicked in and she forced herself to concentrate on Eddie.

'He's been badly burned,' Rhona told them, her voice unsteady. 'He was rushing about to get a lunch order ready and knocked a pan of scalding hot water over his arm. We ran cold water over the burn, but the skin was already peeling away.'

One look at Eddie confirmed the café owner's state of shock and pain. He emerged from the car, shaking and ashen-faced, a sodden towel wrapped over his arm.

'Come on, let's get you inside,' Max said, then turned to Anya. 'We'll take him straight to my room.'

She and Max shared a brief glance that reflected the gravity of the situation. It was as important to get Eddie treated speedily as it was not to shock any of the other patients in the waiting room. Max's decision to take Eddie to his room would save a long detour through the middle of reception to Anya's office at the back of the practice.

'Yes, boss, lead on.'

'You're the burns expert,' Max continued as they helped the patient inside. It proved he'd taken note of her CV. At Cala Muir, Anya was the practice's recognised burns advisor. She'd qualified in burns treatment after working in that area for years post nursing training. She had a special interest in burns; probably because her own mother had suffered burns in her childhood. Marion Fraser had fallen headfirst off a stool into an open coal fire as a child. Her face and neck had been badly scarred.

In normal circumstances, burns would be referred to an Accident and Emergency Department. However, the remote rural nature of their location meant that from time to time emergencies such as this showed up at either of the village's two medical centres. This happened most often at Cala Muir, primarily because Struan had once worked in A&E, and thanks to Anya's burns training. The local hospital for the catchment area was sixty miles away — severe emergency treatment had to be administered via air ambulance.

'I'll need gauze, dressings, cleaning solution and saline,' she told Max. 'Plus ibuprofen for Eddie's discomfort.'

'I'll have someone fetch them immediately. Mr Carsdale, you've come to us in good time. Don't panic, try to relax.'

'This looks like a partial thickness burn,' she said softly to Max. 'The skin appears deep red-purple, swollen and blistered, and there's weeping. It will be extremely painful and hypersensitive.'

She reassured Eddie and his daughter that they had done the right things, which was good news. One should never attempt to burst any blisters that have formed on burnt skin. The first step would be to stop the burning process, carefully remove clothing, and then flood surface areas with cold water until medical help could be sought.

'You did very well, Rhona, in reacting quickly and getting his arm in water. The skin usually swells after a burn so it's important to remove anything constricting it.'

'I took his watch off,' said Rhona.

'Great work. I'm now going to clean the burn gently with cleansing solution, and wash it off with saline. Then I'll remove any loose epidermis and dress the wound. That should establish a sterile environment for healing.' She worked quickly and deftly. 'How are you feeling, Mr Carsdale?'

'Still shocked. But a little better,

thanks. Rhona's shaking now.'

'But getting water on the burn promptly was an excellent move on her part,' Anya countered. 'Rhona, you'd better take a seat. You're in shock. Don't worry, your dad's going to be fine.'

She offered them tea, then left the patient alone with his daughter for a few moments. Eddie's painkillers would take a short while to kick in.

Anya realised in a small pocket of her subconscious that this felt great. Lurching into action to make a real difference in an emergency — it was what her training had been all about.

Only, this time, Max had been watching close by.

★   ★   ★

'Anya, can we talk?' Max asked softly as she turned to leave his consulting room.

Anya pivoted on her heels and peeled off the surgical gloves. 'Sure.'

Eddie Carsdale's burns had been

dressed and he'd been sent home and told to rest, that his wound would be painful for some time and a short period of recuperation was advised. They'd given him another appointment to check on progress.

And Max had watched Anya throughout, impressed and riveted. Noting every reaction, each glance and response. She was bright, efficient, an excellent colleague.

Plus, every movement she made deepened his awareness of her as a woman. Even the way her lower lip pulled when she was anxious or thinking.

Her practical professionalism impressed him. Just seeing her in that utilitarian blue nurse's uniform had him gulping back awareness.

Did she realise the fierce sparks she caused inside him? Did she feel this chemistry too? Or was he going crazy?

'You did well with Eddie. And earlier, too, braving those aviator overalls.' He was trying to coax a smile from her.

'Maybe we should make them compulsory?'

She raised her eyebrows to challenge his judgement. 'Too many zippers. I'd never find my pen. Anyway, fight or flight took hold. That burn could have been much worse. At least they reacted promptly by coming right in.'

Max sat on the edge of the desk. 'The parachuting practice nurse drops in to save the day.'

'Says the heroic daring doctor. We're turning into a comedy duo.'

'And a great team.' Though there was nothing comic about the way he felt about her. Lately, his thoughts kept straying back to this woman. 'So, you think we make a good pair?'

With a brief glance she dismissed his question. Her silence told him everything he needed to know.

Yet Max couldn't bring himself to leave the trail there. 'I've told you how I feel about that already.' He could see from her face that she understood his inference. 'And you always duck away.'

Anya shook her head. Slowly her gaze rose to meet his. 'I'm not ducking. Just keeping a healthy professional distance. I thought you'd understood my position when I said we need established boundaries. I get the feeling you aren't taking me seriously.'

Before he left, Eddie had promised them lunch by way of thanks once normality returned at The Bracken Café. Max hoped he'd be able to pin Anya down on that soon. Her evasion bothered him more than he cared to admit.

Was his attraction too obvious? Was that why she kept avoiding him?

'I take you extremely seriously. You're professional to a fault, and your burns knowledge is a feather in the practice's cap. Professionally, I've hit the jackpot with you. I just wish you didn't act so scared of me all the time.' He managed a smile. 'Can't we just have a quick coffee now to shake all this awkwardness?'

Anya flexed tired shoulders, then

checked her watch. 'I have to pick up Callum soon. Because of Eddie's emergency I've over-run on my surgery hours as it is.'

'I'll ensure you're paid overtime. But I understand if you need to go.'

She shook her head. 'He'll be OK; I already asked Lucy to call my childminder Laura about the emergency with Eddie. Can I make another quick call now? I don't have time for coffee but I can stay to quickly talk things through.'

'I totally understand. Can I give you a lift to the childminder afterwards?'

Anya declined his offer. 'No need,' she replied smoothly. 'Laura's very amenable. And flexible — a real godsend. I'll call her first, then we'll talk.'

She walked off to make her call.

Why did it twist his insides, feeling that her spare time was always in too short supply around him?

Max paced up and down his small office until her return. When he went briefly to reception to retrieve some paperwork, he noticed her talking seriously with Eddie's driver, William Mays, who was still there. According to Lucy the receptionist he'd waited to see her. William had been in the café when the accident happened, and had volunteered to help.

Max recognised a pang of envy at the intimate, hushed manner in which he was talking to Anya. The way the man watched her so intently . . . His practice nurse was definitely a favourite with the public.

When she returned ten minutes later with her jacket and bag, he couldn't resist asking, 'William OK?'

He saw colour rise on her complexion. 'He's back from overseas. He suggested dinner; he never gets the message.'

Max felt envy flicker but pulled his thoughts away, his mental suspicion confirmed. 'Is he making a nuisance of himself?'

Anya shook her head. 'So, let's discuss boundaries.'

It was a window of opportunity. He had Anya all to himself, and time enough to clear the air.

'I feel like you're avoiding me,' he began. 'I've hardly seen you around. I want to apologise if I've misunderstood how things stand between us.'

Max sat on the desk instead of behind it, watching her reaction.

Was she so diligent that she barely crossed the threshold of her office? Did she go for lunch off the premises every *single* day? She'd been ducking away every time their paths crossed, seeming to head in the opposite direction whenever he hoped to snatch an opportunity for a chat. She was playing the studious nurse card but it felt like a switch had been turned off between them.

He must have come on too strong that night at her cottage. That possibility bothered him. Even the brief 'Thank you!' she'd given him on Katie's behalf — so brief it had been a sprint dash — had been hastily delivered, as if Anya

109

was frightened he might bite her.

'I've been busy,' she said defensively. With interest, he noted her blush. 'But I'm also aware that you're my boss. This is a small village, and people talk. I want to get the balance right.' She hesitated. 'How are you settling in, anyway?'

'Fine. A bit heavy on the admin workload at the moment, but I'll soon be up to speed. Anya, please believe me, I won't do anything to make you feel awkward.'

Right now it was the woman who was worrying him more than the job teething gripes.

'Perhaps I didn't make myself clear enough the other night,' she murmured. 'We're colleagues, and that's our priority.'

'The other night, I didn't mean to offend you. Being so frank about my past.'

'You didn't, Max. But I think it's best for both of us if there's professional space between us. I shouldn't have kissed you. Your comment today made me worry that I've already blurred the lines.'

'It was intended and taken as a friendly peck. And I heard what you said loud and clear. Today I was just being flippant to ease your fears about the photocall, and I got it wrong. I'm sorry for that. Sometimes humour gets lost in translation.'

'So I did make myself plain when we talked at the cottage. I'm not ready for a relationship,' she confirmed, biting her lip. 'I had second thoughts that maybe I'd encouraged you unduly. I'm not in the market for dating, Max. It's only fair that you realise that. I haven't room in my life for a man.'

Max nodded slowly. Even though he now realised he found her seriously attractive, he had to respect her honesty. As senior partner — and as a guy who viewed this nurse as someone worth taking especially good care of — he had to take her at her word.

'Well, I'm still here as a friend if you

need one. Though you're such a vibrant woman. Surely closing yourself off to a social life is a waste?'

'I have a social life. Maybe limited by some standards, but it suits me fine.'

'If I thought my coming here had made you feel awkward at work, I'd never forgive myself. Tell me truthfully, have I upset you?'

He hoped his sincerity showed in his eyes.

'I'll be honest with you.' Anya shifted uncomfortably in her seat. 'I wasn't impressed with your flirty asides today. It's hard enough working together without you saying such inappropriate things. You're the new senior partner. So please don't make things hard for me. And respect the fact that I don't want a relationship. After all, maybe turning you down is hard for me.'

She said it in such a way that it made his insides thrum with hope. Was it possible she was finding it hard to turn him down?

'I was honestly trying to make you

laugh and talk to me. However unsubtle and schoolboyish my efforts have been. I'm sorry if I've offended you. But don't write us off like this. Give me a chance? I won't let you down.'

She sighed. 'I'd rather we were businesslike at work.'

'I'm sorry, I'm making a hash of things.'

He rose briefly and paced the room.

Anya pivoted to view him and their gazes met. 'Let's just try and be normal around each other, Max. Being friends is fine. As long as lines don't blur.'

'I think we could have something special together. And the fact you feel it too leaves me determined to make you see you're wasting an opportunity here.'

'I'm not ready to risk Cal's security to go over old ground with a new boyfriend.'

Max reached out and stroked her arm. 'I give you my word I won't hurt you. I only want to make you happy.'

'Give me time, Max. I'm not making

any promises; all I can handle right now is friendship and relaxed good times.'

Max burned to reach out and take her hand in his, but did not want to ruin the tentative trust they had built together here.

'Gemma's invitation to dinner. She asks if we can make it next Friday?' Max chanced instead.

He hoped she'd accept. He was willing her to say yes. The offhand evasiveness of the last few days had bugged him. He wanted to sort things out and start getting to know her.

'I'll have to get a babysitter arranged before I can confirm,' she said firmly. 'Leave it with me.'

He rose from his perch on the desk. 'One other thing — would you like to go out for a drink with me beforehand? Just social chat. And I'll be on my best behaviour.'

She seemed to weigh it up. No doubt thinking of some good, pressing excuse to turn him down.

'You can think that over too if you

like,' he added. 'No rush. I've learned my lesson.'

She stood up. 'Katie promised she could babysit anytime. What harm can a social dinner and a drink at the pub do? Though not local, if that's OK. Tongues wag, and I'd rather they didn't.'

He stretched out a hand to her. 'No avoiding me at work from now on? Friends?'

'Friends,' she agreed, before turning for the door. 'I have to go. Night, Max.'

Her eyes held his before she disappeared; blue and grey velvet worlds of delight. And now he could rest in the knowledge he'd be looking into them again soon.

'She said yes; don't blow it,' he said to himself, starting to whistle as he faced the case notes on his desk. It might not be the Anya in jeans on a bike fantasy in his head, but together in a cosy corner of a country pub would be more than enough for now.

7

'Mummy, is that really you?'

Callum's plaintive, incredulous tone drew Anya up; even at age four, disbelief lurked beneath.

She watched him point to the large colour photograph on the front page of the Craig Inch, Glenshiel Chronicle and scowl quizzically.

'Why are you wearing those things on your head?'

'They're goggles,' Anya explained patiently. 'People wear them when they jump out of aeroplanes. Mummy's going to do that soon to make money for Katie's work, and that's what I'm going to be wearing.'

She could tell from the look on her young son's face the explanation hadn't computed but she didn't know how to put it more simply.

It was indeed her on the front page

of their local newspaper. Along with Max, Katie and Tina, smiling into the camera lens as if she was au fait with mid-air life-threatening behaviour and not trembling at the very thought. The banner headline read — *Medics Make Charity Leap, Show Your Support!*

And in the middle, Max smiled like a hero in some blockbuster action movie. It made her heart tremble just to look at him.

She was still groaning inwardly when her son went back to his crayoning.

She thought of all her patients' comments — stray jokes at her expense and asides such as '*Oh, it's Anya — dropping in from on high?*' wherever she went in the village. It would be worth it though if they agreed to support their cause. She vowed that all clever asides would warrant an immediate sponsorship pledge penalty. That would soon shut them all up.

Anya picked up the newspaper and carried it through to the kitchen with her; and then, as her eye scanned the story copy her stomach went on freefall. Her breath caught in her chest.

She was quoted, and the piece featured her name and address. It missed out a street number but it clearly stated the tiny street her cottage was located in. And there were only two other cottages beside hers. How hard would it be to find her, given half a pinch of common sense? What if this private information fell into the hands of Callum's birth parents?

Anya Fraser, Cala Muir Medical Centre's Practice Nurse of Whin Wynd, Alderwick Loch, said, 'Frankly I'm terrified even going up a ladder! But this charity fundraiser has such a worthy cause it's worth mastering my fears for. The charity stands to benefit local people, children, prospective adopters and families needing support post placement. Please give all you can to make this event a success.'

The letters swam before her eyes in black and white newsprint.

So much for her prized anonymity.

Now she felt regret at her foolhardy actions. She also felt a distinct trickle of fear. The thought of anything jeopardising the life she'd fought so hard for with her son was excruciating. She deserved Cal, didn't she? She'd been patient, dealt with the grief of not being able to have a child of her own. She'd been through so much. The thought of her situation being challenged by some foolish slip in a newspaper report pained her.

Why had she agreed to this nonsense anyhow? Why had she even ventured near anything that could compromise her identity?

The telephone rang nearby and Anya answered with a brusque, 'What is it?'

She hoped it would be Katie so she could fire the array of questions that were zipping through her head. How had the newspaper got her details?

'Anya?' The male voice paused. 'It's Max. Are you alright?'

'Have you seen the local paper?

'Seen it!' he replied, and she could

hear the smile in his voice. 'I've been signing copies for patients all morning. This notoriety's wearing thin already. The money's coming thick and fast, though.'

She interrupted him. 'This is serious, Max. I'm not happy about it, I'm in a panic.'

There was a further pause down the line and Anya looked back down at the garish photograph that even now was making her angry.

'Tell me what's happened.'

'My name and address have been mentioned.'

She could hear the rustle of newspaper sheets down the line. 'You're right. I hadn't even picked that up. But Katie's address appears too . . . ?'

'I should never have agreed to this. Callum's anonymity has always been paramount to me.'

'But *he* isn't mentioned.'

'Back before Callum was placed, I met his birth parents. They know my first name and what I look like. His father was dangerous, and collectively they fought the adoption. Having me as front-page news with the street I live in makes me feel highly vulnerable.'

'Do Callum's birth parents live locally?'

'No, they're in another region.'

'Then there's no panic, then,' Max said calmingly, soothing her slightly because he sounded so assured and confident of his facts. 'This is a local newspaper with a limited circulation. I understand your fears, and they're totally justified, but I honestly wouldn't worry. I think the chance of them seeing this is remote.'

'Well, I'm not so convinced.'

'I realise you've had a shock. I imagine them putting in your street was a mistake, though I know putting street names in is newspaper policy.'

'Katie told me this piece would be anonymous.'

'I can make enquiries in the surgery — though I'm sure no-one on the staff would have released your details out of data protection stringency.'

'The damage is done now.'

And just then something made sense in a dark corner of her brain. Anya suddenly realised how her details might have become public; she knew a trainee reporter at the Chronicle, a nephew of her neighbour Fiona Young.

Could it be that Ryan had recognised her? He'd contacted her himself in the past for information on local health stories. She would put money on this being the reason.

'Try to stay calm about this mix-up. We're in a remote village with a tiny local paper. You're right to be protective of Callum, but I think in this case it'll be fine. You've as much chance of being recognised through the practice notice boards and the patients' newsletters as through this. I know it's hard not to worry. A mother's instincts, and all . . .'

Anya sighed and rubbed at her temple. 'Thanks, Max. I'll try.'

He was right, wasn't he? She was

overreacting. And there was something in the way Max talked — caressing her senses, easing her with his calm, confident assurances — that helped her see how much she had blown this out of proportion.

'OK,' she agreed. 'Let's hope it's worth it and we boost funds.'

'That's why I called. Besides wanting to speak to you, of course.'

'Flattery will get you everywhere.'

'Am I back in your good books?' he joked. 'I've been on my best behaviour at work lately, did you notice?'

She suppressed an inner smile. 'I noticed. What about the sponsorship?'

'A rep from a drugs company came in today and pledged an impressive contribution. He's also asked if he can take part. And the director of the local health authority saw the piece, and he's agreed to pledge support. So, all in all — great work. I've already called Katie to let her know, and she's thrilled.'

'That's fantastic.'

'Are you still on for Friday's dinner

at Gemma's?' he asked. His tones seemed to change from casual to intent and intimate. Or was she imagining that? No, definitely intimate — like they had a shared secret and he enjoyed that.

'I asked Katie to babysit, but she told me she couldn't make it; then my mum offered to take Callum for the night.'

Anya realised she might have revealed too much. She'd intended to keep that to herself. Not that she imagined Max Calder would take advantage of her, but she didn't want him to think she was clearing the way for nightcaps.

'I'm still not sure if Callum staying with her overnight is such a good idea. He struggles with change.'

Her son would love the treat. The problem was that such moves involving adopted kids sometimes caused problems. Even brief overnight changes or holidays needed full preparation, or they could bring difficult behaviours and upset. Children with a lot of change in their early years were highly susceptible to altered routines.

Then again, she couldn't protect Callum from change for the rest of his life, could she?

'I hope you do make it. I thought we could drive out to the Crofter's Yard for a pre-dinner chat. As a reward for my good behaviour at work.'

She smiled. He had, it was true, been exemplary, as a new senior partner should be; he always greeted her in a friendly but brisk manner. Didn't loiter when they met. He'd displayed admirable brevity in all matters.

'It feels like you've been at Cala Muir forever.'

'I told you, I'm a great actor. Off duty, I'm even more impressive.' His tone was cheeky.

She laughed aloud.

'Mummy, come and see the drawing I've made of you in your goggles.' Cal's voice was insistent as he tugged on her sleeve.

'I have to go.'

'Fine, see you Friday. At seven?'

'Yes. Thanks for talking me round

today. I needed it.'

'Any time.'

Anya went off to inspect Cal's crayon drawing. A picture in which she'd be looking fearless, heroic, and unafraid of heights.

Little did any of them know . . .

★   ★   ★

The topic of Anya's questionable suitability for parachute jumping came up the following day when her mum called her at work.

'Have you miraculously mastered your fear of heights without telling me? The paper says a *parachute* jump. Are you mad?'

She feigned being bright and breezy, clicking her pen with every pulse jump. 'I meant to tell you. I'm being sponsored to do it. With an instructor, so don't worry — I'm raising money for charity.'

'I read the article. But you won't do it, surely?' Her mother's lack of faith sounded in every clipped word.

'I fully intend to.' It irked her that her mother had such shallow vision.

'Have you told Katie and the others about your history? Do they realise the severity of your aversion?'

Since she was eight years old and had gone to an activity park featuring a high rope ladder, she'd found heights difficult. Meaning she became short of breath and panicky, verging on the dizziness of vertigo if she went too close to the edge. But, while she'd avoided heights as far as possible during her life, now was the time to face things. For the greater good. Or so Anya had felt before the phone call from her mother.

Plus, it was time to give something back to the charity that had been her salvation. That was her major motivation.

Having an irrational fear didn't mean she couldn't try to address it, and wasn't a charity skydive a perfect opportunity?

To think she was the woman who'd nagged and lectured Grant because of his risky weekend hobby of rally driving. It had nearly sent her crazy when he went out on each weekend rally, often in bad weather. And now, here she was, sky-diving.

'Well, I hope you're right. And that this jumping-from-a-plane notion isn't an embarrassing mistake.'

Even though her mother's comment stabbed at the balloon of her optimism, she forced her spine straight. She flexed her fingers and pulled the phone cord tight, then turned her eyes on Callum's smiling photograph.

'I want to prove I can get over old hang-ups. It's time I challenged and conquered it.'

'You know you're not a risk-taker. Why would you decide to confront this now?'

'Trust me. I know what I'm doing.'

'Your father would have disapproved,' Marion Fraser said, sounding wary. 'It's one thing being a good sport for charity, but you don't want to put yourself in a hazardous situation.'

The mention of her father, who'd died prior to Callum's placement, was a sore point for Anya. He'd treated her with kid gloves over her aversion to heights. And other things — like his blind refusal to accept her inability to conceive. It was as if he felt any problem brought weakness. He'd never discussed it with her, nor expressed any compassion.

Anya bit her lip. Max had confidence in her, didn't he? He was the confident, cool, composed daredevil who took charge with ease.

'I've got an excellent tutor. I'm confident I'll prove you wrong,' she told her mother with finality. 'He believes in me and I trust him. Please just believe that I can do this and let me try.'

If anyone could help her get over this fear of heights, Max could.

* * *

Max woke up at dawn in his room, sweating like he was on safari, only this was much worse. His heart raced; he felt hoarse with panic. He'd been running, scared; transported back to thorny, bleak childhood years.

Why now?

Was it Anya?

Had hearing her fears about a birth father catching up with her rattled him subconsciously?

He'd forgotten what it felt to experience that kind of unfettered fear. That loathing and hatred and the racing adrenaline of fighting with a greater force than you.

His dad had been coming at him with a broom. The gnarled broom that looked like it had been hand-hewn to terrify. The end of the handle had been destined to leather whatever part of him came first. Until there were welts on the back of his buttocks and legs bigger than oak tree leaves.

The broom was a primary indicator that Dad was having a bad day.

130

'Come here, you, this time you're for it,' Robert Calder would snarl fiercely.

He remembered the big guy's hands. Like dinner plates. Wide and fat, leathery too. Max knew why he'd have been a great miner — hands like that were built to hew coal. They could beat a son as easily as they could smash into the hard mineral earth.

'I'm coming nowhere,' Max had said, half defiant, half panic-stricken. Even in the dream he'd heard a young voice inside him reply, shrill panic behind the cry. There was no way he was going anywhere near those hands. Not if he could help it. The same hands that only a week before had burned him with a cigarette for getting into bother running around with the local gang.

'You're coming here, and I'll flog you good and hard. So help me, I'll show you a lesson, boy!'

Those were the last words he remembered his dad saying in the dream before he woke, sweating, shaking like a little kid. And he a man of past thirty, and now bigger and burlier than his dad had ever been in his lifetime.

He knew Robert Calder was six feet under. Best place for him, too.

Max crossed to the bedroom dresser and poured a glass of water from the bottle there. He drank deeply and rubbed his mouth with the back of his arm.

'That adoption charity jump. Bringing back hidden memories. It has to be,' he told himself quietly. 'Or you're cracking up, Calder.'

The phone buzzed and he picked it up. It was a callout to a pregnant patient in Byreside Fields; he knew her husband from football, and though he suspected it might be Braxton Hicks contractions rather than oncoming labour, it paid to check. Max was only ten minutes' drive away.

Swiftly, he got dressed, glad to escape the dreams of his past. Sometimes, he was never quite sure if his 'daring' tagline was a cover for his dark inner fear.

*   *   *

'Dinner's off,' Max told her. 'Gemma Stuart's husband Sean has got a nasty viral infection. He's throwing up violently. I've done a house call.'

He was standing in her office doorway, looking way too gorgeous. Pale grey shirt, well-cut charcoal chinos, shiny leather shoes to match his shiny head of thick, short, just-cut hair. The desirable doctor personified.

'Poor guy,' said Anya sympathetically.

But of course, if Sean was ill, there was no question of the dinner going ahead.

'I've got an alternative plan,' he said, his eyes glittering. 'The pre-dinner drink at the pub still stands. Then back to my place for a meal? Shame to waste a good babysitting arrangement.'

Anya did not know what to say, though she was tempted to go for *Yes*.

His smile ensnared her. 'Please?' he added. 'I could beg; but if I do, I'd rather you locked your office door first in case someone catches me.'

She laughed and shook her head. 'A friendly dinner sounds OK. As long as you promise not to keep lobbying for more.'

'Naturally.' He bowed gallantly, then threw her a wink. 'I'm very well behaved, and I've a reputation in this community to uphold.'

'And don't go to too much trouble on my behalf. It's only casual.'

He raised an eyebrow. 'There is a stipulation.' When she shot him a quizzical look, he smiled. 'I intend to take you out to the pub on my bike. Ever ridden on a touring bike before, Ms Fraser? Best to wear jeans.'

'Wow. You are intent on pushing my boundaries, aren't you?'

'Pick you up at seven. Remember to dress for the bike.'

'Max, can I ask you something?' she added hurriedly as he turned to leave.

'Height aversion. Have you ever tutored a parachute jumper who finds climbing a ladder to paint the ceiling a problem?'

'Really? You?' The surprise showed in his face.

She nodded with sincerity. 'I still want to do this. I want to overcome the fear. As it's for a good cause, it seems like a heaven-sent opportunity.'

Max said with a nod, 'I'm sure I can try my best to make a skydiver of you. Leave it with me; we'll talk later. You're in good hands — so try to relax.'

With a wide smile, Max turned and left — but she couldn't erase the memory of that smile. Not for the entire afternoon.

Max was on her side. And she was about to go on a biker-girl date with him.

* * *

Could life be any better?

Yeah. He supposed it could. He could have pulled Anya into his arms and kissed those just-glossed lips. For now, he'd settle for a date at the pub.

Sean Stuart was laid up in bed, yellow-faced and groaning from a chronic case of the Norovirus winter vomiting bug.

The irksome virus caused sickness, diarrhoea and fever and typically lasted from twenty-four to forty-eight hours. Sean had called in Max on a home visit, primarily in view of Isla's frequent ill health and the risks to her. Plus, Sean being the head chef at a local hotel, he was in constant contact with food.

During his home visit, Max had told Sean that if someone with the bug was sick, the virus could end up in aerosol form on surrounding surfaces and objects. So Max had instructed Sean and Gemma that the most important basic point with the virus was strict hygiene. Gemma had vowed to be stringent in view of Isla's immune system deficiencies.

'Yes!' said Max, going back to his office. 'Roll on, my date. Get well soon,

Sean. But thanks for the advantage, buddy.'

Then he buzzed his next patient into the room, firmly pushing away the stray thrilling fantasy about holding Anya close in that dark medical supplies cupboard down the hall.

'Steady!' he schooled himself. 'All in good time.'

8

When Anya found herself changing prior to her dinner with Max it was after a hectic week of work, work and more work.

The local Alderwick Community had been awash with viral issues to contend with, so time sped quickly by. Two local nurseries had reported conjunctivitis doing the rounds. It had caused extra work administering advice and treating the sore eyes of young patients. There was also an outbreak of impetigo at the local secondary school — a painful and infectious skin condition

As she brushed her hair and put on a touch of make-up, that sneaky sense of caution crept back in spite of the casual approach to their assignation.

Was she crazy, going out with the boss so soon?

Even her casual jeans outfit did little

to allay the feeling that there was more to this evening than a relaxed, informal meal. She felt it inside like a low electric current.

She planned special little touches to her outfit in spite of the 'casual' stipulation. A sharp tailored white shirt worn with a stone choker necklace, pointed toe boots, and a faux leather jacket she saved for the rock chick look. She could still go to a little effort, couldn't she?

Her mother had picked Callum up at six, breezing in busy as ever with the promise of a DVD that had Cal jumping up and down like a jack-in-the-box in anticipation. Little did her mum suspect — Anya had told her she was going out with a couple of girls from work for a drink, and while a smidge of guilt tugged at her for the lie, she wasn't prepared to share the truth with her mother yet. That would involve questions, maybe a shocked look at the revelation. Public knowledge of her innocent plans with Max could wait.

The doorbell rang. Max stood on the doorstep, smiling and bearing two helmets for the bike, one in each hand. He looked fantastic in great-fitting faded dark jeans, his crisp baby-blue shirt open to reveal a glimpse of chest.

'I brought you this,' he said with a smile, presenting the helmet, 'though on second thoughts maybe flowers would have been a touch more considerate. You ready? Not too early?'

'As I'll ever be!' she answered. 'If you promise you won't go too fast. I am a beginner, after all. Be gentle with me.'

'Special cargo — I'll take utmost care. I'll even let you enjoy the views.'

Just seeing him had the excited winged insects in her tummy tilting and tipping and flying around as if circling a hurricane lamp. She hadn't seen her favourite senior partner all day. Lately, everyone at Cala Muir enjoyed his company. She hadn't seen much of him; it was as if fate was keeping them at a safe distance. Or driving her a little crazy in the lead-up to tonight.

Only not seeing Max made her wonder about him more, made her mind float off to find him in her fantasies, imagining him in situ behind his big beech desk. His long legs stretched and loafers tapping the floor as she'd noticed he did when he was distracted. She found herself wondering how he was with patients, and whether he was charming them as he introduced himself into practice life.

'So you don't mind that I omitted the flowers?' he asked as she locked her cottage.

'The helmet's a much more safety-conscious option. And it doesn't need a vase of water, either.'

He walked her to the bike and helped her on. Up close, with her hands tucked around his firm midriff on the bike — her thighs just touching his rear — it felt intimate. *Calm down*, she told herself. It was a necessary bike-riding manoeuvre. But she still couldn't help the way it made her words wobble in her chest or her breathing dip.

'OK?' he asked through the helmet.

'I think so.'

Max squeezed her knee.

'Relax.'

He advised her not to sit rigidly, but to mould herself to the bike's movements. It felt strange at first, particularly going around corners, but in only a few minutes she felt her anxieties and posture start to loosen.

It had to be said, riding pillion was exhilarating. As buzz inducing as jumping out of a plane with a parachute, she wondered? With Max there, anything was possible.

Max gave her a thumbs-up when they stopped at the lights.

'*Casual date at a pub in jeans,*' she chanted mentally like a mantra.

She wondered what Callum or her mother would say if they could see her now. Or her workmates at the surgery. They'd stare after them with open mouths. She was grateful the helmets had smoky visors to conceal their identities. And suddenly it was great living a different life from her normal day-to-day sensible routine. Adrenaline pumping hard in her veins.

She gave way to a giggle, which Max must have sensed, because he turned slightly to cast her a quick glance.

He'd promised her an enjoyable ride tonight.

What else did Dr. Max Calder have up his daredevil's sleeve?

* * *

After a thirty-minute ride out into the wilds of the Scottish countryside, Max pulled up outside the Crofter's Yard. It was an infamous pub, but luckily not too local to Alderwick so as to be full of locals recognising her from surgery life. The pub served fantastic food, and their ale and malts were award-winning. It also had ancient origins, being built on a turnpike road, so it had garnered a legend with tourists as a haunted hostelry.

They dismounted and removed their helmets. Anya's hair products were somewhat wasted on the windswept style which emerged from her helmet.

'What did you think of the bike?'

She laughed. 'It's a definite hair challenge, but a fresh-air way to travel.'

'I'm glad you enjoyed it.' His smile could fell derelict buildings.

'*Enjoyed*'s a bit strong,' she warned. 'Let's just say it's bearable.'

'But you like it here?'

'Very much. My favourite place for grilled trout.'

'Now you're talking,' said Max with a grin. 'That's good, as I've had to change plans. I was late at the surgery, and had no time to get the ingredients I'd planned for dinner. So the trout may be a contender.'

'Great!' said Anya, and felt Max cup her elbow to lead her inside.

'You don't mind eating here?'

'Not at all,' she assured him.

'Much better than my home cooking.'

Max guided her through the expansive saloon bar and nodded to Archie

Muir behind the bar. 'Go through, Max, it's all ready for you!' Archie instructed.

Max thanked him, and led the way through a door she'd never even noticed before, and would have assumed was private.

It led up an ancient spiral staircase and out into a panelled room with intricate ceiling pictures that made Anya gasp as soon as she saw them. The images were of tiny figures involved in some sort of pagan rite — dancing around bonfires, involved in merrymaking. It reminded her of the kind of etchings she'd seen in an illustrated book of Robert Burns's poetry, in particular those accompanying the tale of Tam O'Shanter's brush with the Devil. She'd never seen a room like this in her life.

But the painting wasn't all that the room could boast. Its amazing views of the mountains and local shoreline were breathtaking.

'You said you wanted privacy. How's

this for different?' Max nodded a dark eyebrow in the direction of the landscape beyond the glass.

'I didn't mean you to go to any trouble.'

'It seemed the obvious choice: the secret crypt at the Crofter's. Not everybody knows about it. So I have to initiate you into the special clan.' He said this so seriously that Anya's face must have showed her concern. 'It's OK, I'm not going to ask you to drink spiked malt and dance around the room like a witch. You have to repeat a phrase after me,' Max said, and laughed. 'Say — *I'm off duty and I'm going to enjoy myself.* Repeat this sentence twice!'

She smiled, then repeated it as ordered. He was nothing if not charming, and he knew exactly how to beat down her barricades of formality.

'What are these pictures?' she asked, staring up at the ceiling.

'That depends on whether or not you believe the legend. Some say they're the work of witches. That a coven left them as a record of witchcraft here in the old days. Others say a landlord a few generations back had someone draw them as provenance to the hauntings claim.'

'Then why hide them away up here?'

'The local magistrate threatened to close the place if this kind of witchery was on public view. Hence the secret room. So now you're one of a privileged few. A crofters' 'witchery convert'.'

The craggy, majestic hills and sparkling indigo coastline drew Anya to the windows to take it all in.

'I've booked this room a few times when we've run seminars for visiting medics at my old practice, and once when I had friends over from New Zealand. They loved all the local lore, an authentic touch to their stay. Maybe a weird choice for a date, but I hoped I might show you something you'd never seen before.'

He'd certainly succeeded there. And she was glad she'd seen this room and stood beneath the large ceiling fresco. It felt like a magical mystery tour. The fact that Max cared enough to intrigue her and had put so much effort into their first night out together made her feel special.

'Come on,' Max urged her. 'Tell me what you'd like for dinner and I'll order it. Then we'll sit on the window seat and have a drink. And we can decide exactly what's going on above us. Personally, I've a few theories I'd like to run past you! Some more wicked than others.'

He smiled roguishly.

If there was any witchery going on in this room, half of it was from her own mischievous date. He had the most surprising courting strategies she'd ever encountered.

Was he putting a spell on her too?

'Now, what can I tempt you with?' He waved a menu under her nose. 'Take your time choosing. Unless you're going for your favourite again?'

Even though she'd already decided on the fish, she deliberately took her time, reading the menu, savouring the choices.

She was starting to enjoy herself — much, much more than she'd imagined.

★ ★ ★

'I think you have an admirer,' Max told her in a solemn whisper.

He slid in beside her, carrying two tall iced drinks from the bar. So close, he could breathe deep and smell her bewitching perfume.

'Pardon?' She stared at him oddly.

'William Mays — the guy who came with Eddie Carsdale when he was burned, who drove him to the surgery? He's downstairs at the bar. He saw you come in with me and was asking after you. He wanted to know what you were doing out with me.'

Anya shook her head. 'I've known William a long time, but there's no spark there, trust me. And I think you're wrong. We don't know each other that well. He asked me out for dinner in the past, but always took it well when I refused.'

Max smiled. 'Well, I'm reserving judgement. He seems pretty interested to me. Trust another guy to have a nose for such things.'

In truth, he'd been on the verge of asking William, *Who the heck are you to quiz?*

'I think your imagination is playing tricks on you.' She smiled and sipped her drink sweetly.

'Modest as ever.' He whispered, 'Can I ask you another question? A personal one?'

'Go ahead. I can always decline to answer.'

He'd brought her to this witch folklore place because he hoped to weave a spell oh her. Yet she had him intrigued with her own brand of enchantment.

'Why did you want to adopt, if it's not too personal?'

Anya stared off into the distance, her

blue-grey eyes narrowing.

'For me, it was an easy choice. My sister was a social worker, and for years I've been aware of the heartaches involved in children-and-families work. That the kids waiting on new adoptive families in today's society are generally in that position through criminality or neglect. It's no longer a queue of single mothers giving up babies because of social stigma.'

'So the criminality aspect didn't put you off?' Max countered.

'My ex-partner Grant tried to put me off because of the criminality side. Ironic, considering he was a policeman himself. He felt I might be overstepping my abilities, but my heart was already sold on making an adopted child part of my family by then. The more I learned, the more I knew I had to do it.'

The more layers he peeled away, the more he wanted to investigate. The very things that would have scared other people away seemed to challenge her. She was amazing. Inspiring. Admirable.

He was hooked, needing to discover more of what was under her veneer.

She continued, and he listened intently. 'I was never deterred. It makes the plight of the kids who wait all the more poignant. They need new homes because the ones they have can't protect them. Who could fail to be affected by that? And why would I want to investigate other ways to have a baby myself when there are kids in dire need of someone to care for them?'

'But your ex didn't feel the same?'

She shook her head. 'Grant was a policeman. He had his sights on promotion and went for a traffic police job in Glasgow without my knowledge. He was starting to feel life in Alderwick Loch was too tame. When he got the job, he explained it was his ultimate dream, so we started to make arrangements to move to the city together. Halfway through finding a flat there, I realised that I loved my home village and didn't want to leave. In the end, we went in separate directions.'

'That must've been tough,' said Max. 'And I'm guessing your ex is now happily promoted to his dream job and living in Glasgow?'

Anya seemed to tense. She looked away and shook her head. 'Grant died shortly afterwards.'

He felt winded, blindsided by her frankness.

'I'm sorry.'

'He was at work, chasing joyriders who were running amok through the city centre streets. The roads were wet and dangerous. Grant was a pro driver, but he collided with a lorry on the wrong side of the road. He didn't survive. Poor Grant. At least he took the path he wanted, he seized the dream. Even though it ended so cruelly.'

Max stayed silent.

Anya had weathered harsh storms indeed. Baby desires unrequited. A lover who had yearned for new adventures, and then lost his life in tragic circumstances. She'd had it tough.

'Have I just wrecked our date?' he asked, with remorse in his voice.

'No,' she answered. 'It happened. It's in the past. Life isn't always rosy and full of smiles as we both well know.'

'Callum has lived up to your expectations, though. He's brightened your life.' Max tried to lift the sombre mood he'd created unwittingly.

Her smile was triumphant, all maternal pride and delight in response.

'Callum's my everything. He put all the bad bits right. I can't imagine life without him. But can I ask you a question back?' she asked. 'How do you feel about not staying with your birth family? If you don't want to answer, that's fine.'

Max loved the way Anya understood the whole adoption process stuff. She was so grounded, resilient and remarkable. She understood.

Part of the reason he kept his own heritage and dysfunctional family to himself was not because he was ashamed. Usually people didn't get what he'd been through. Or they felt pity. Or wanted details. Details that were strictly private territory only.

'I feel lucky because I got a second chance,' he replied, as honestly as he could. 'But it still hurts.'

'As an adoptive mother, I can only hope Callum's as philosophical about it.'

'Most people don't understand how social services intervention works. They think kids get new futures and names overnight like in the musical *Annie*. They feel sorry for the kids, or think they should be grateful. I have complex feelings about my past that I never expect anyone to get. My heritage is a two-sided thing: good and bad.'

'Chaotic but still yours. You resent people making assumptions.'

'Exactly. What right have they got?'

'None.'

'Most people wouldn't understand why I resisted being made to leave my birth family and kept running away from my Aunt Violet in the early days.

They'd think I was a reprobate. In reality, I was scared witless. I resented the enforced nature of it.'

'You clearly dealt with a lot. You showed a bravery most people have no idea about.'

'I wasn't brave. There were some things about my past I'm immensely proud of, but other things that deeply shame me. I put my aunt through a lot of worry, and all she ever tried to do was help me.'

Aunt Violet had made him feel his own worth through her patient, unconditional love. She'd seen the spark of intellect inside him, and almost dared him to try and realise it. Aunt Violet had never used force or lecturing. She'd seen beyond the feisty, troublesome kid, and realised that the route to achieving the best out of Max was to let him choose his own path. And he'd done it in his own time.

Ironic to think that he'd wanted to stay in that hellhole because it had been all he'd known.

Max looked into blue-grey eyes that stared at his over the table. Empathetic eyes devoid of pity. Full of wit, understanding and courageous grit.

He'd told her all that aloud.

He hadn't intended to, but knew that he had. The words had tumbled out — and this was supposed to be a date!

'I've never told anyone those things.'

She reached across to take his hand. 'Talking's good, Max. Take it from someone who bottled her emotions inside for too long. It's great to let it out. It's the only way to leave it behind.'

Of course, Max knew there were some things he couldn't share with her. Like his fears over what he might have inherited from his father's genes. Was there a selfish bully inside him too?

He was well-educated and had respect for humanity. But he still loved to escape the humdrum working life and throw himself around from a great height to feel the buzz of risking his neck.

He loved to stare at death, to take

high risks and beat them. Was this something his father had bred into him because of his chaotic, wild-riding past?

'Can I ask you a question?' she ventured, interrupting his thoughts, and he smiled.

'Shoot.'

'Why have you never married, Max?'

He shrugged and his lips pulled into an expression of uncertainty. 'Never met the right woman. Never slowed down enough to try my luck. Never ever planned on settling down. Probably because my parents showed me their version of a relationship nightmare. Who'd want to revisit that?'

9

Max wasn't secure future material; he was telling Anya that himself. She couldn't fault him for his honesty. And yet tonight she was warming to him even more, getting to know what lay beneath. But she could also tell when someone was bluffing.

Max bluffed like a pro. She knew where he'd developed that skill from. He'd already told her more about his childhood than she'd ever imagined he would.

She'd seen the dull ache in his eyes when she'd asked him about marriage. She knew it was an ache because it was the same look she'd mastered when she handled questions like, 'When are you and Grant going to have a family? Any news on the patter of tiny feet yet?'

She'd seen the hurt that lurked beneath that look of his. The evasion and skirting around the corners of the truth.

Only, what was he hiding? Hurt? Fear? Disappointment? Why was a long-term future with a partner a no-no for the handsome Cala Muir senior partner?

She felt sure he was hiding the truth. Anya knew, because she'd done that herself often. Losing control of something in your life that mattered greatly — powerlessness mingled with shock — had the ability to do that. Despite their differing situations, she empathised with him and his habit of dodging the truth.

Max changed the subject and headed her off by going to fetch more drinks.

Then, right in the middle of dinner, which they'd agreed several times was exquisite, he made his shocking admission.

'I need to make a confession.'

Anya's gaze lingered on him. 'Confession?' She pulled a quizzical face.

'I lied. I didn't work late at the

surgery. I could have bought the ingredients for my casserole, and the expensive bottle of wine is, even as we speak, sitting in my kitchen. But I lied. I wanted to take you out.'

Not a good sign. She didn't admire men who twisted truths to suit their own ends. Hadn't Grant done that? Left her ignorant as to his interview in Glasgow? He'd kept her in the dark because his own needs came first.

'Why?'

'To avoid talking about my past. Crazy, isn't it? Which is the thing I've done of my own volition. I wanted to bring you out to dinner. I was worried that if I asked you straight out, you'd bolt. You sometimes look like you're very wary and are hoping for a hasty escape. So I lied to get you here.' Max bit his lip. 'Do you mind?'

Maybe he could be forgiven when he put it like that?

She fancied Max Calder the man. She enjoyed Max the guy's company. She marvelled at Max the GP's admirable professionalism. Now she was falling for Max the adopted little boy. Lethal.

Anya fixed him with the kind of stern stare that did a great job on her son when he'd been up to no good. 'I have that murky secret of my own, remember.'

He nodded. 'Oh yes, the heights problem.'

'This parachute jump,' she agreed. 'I'm scared witless at the prospect. I must have been mad ever to agree to it. You see, I'm afraid of heights. I'm badly affected. Even as a child, going up in lifts left me dizzy. At first, I thought saying yes to the skydive would be a good way of conquering my fears, but now I'm worried about *not* doing it, and even more scared about going ahead and throwing myself from a plane. I owe it to the charity to pull through and conquer this.'

Max reached out to touch her hand. 'We'll get you through it.'

'Katie's so persuasive, and the charity

needs the money so badly, and now I feel like a fool. What will people say if I back out?'

'You're no fool. I think it's brave to confront your fear. So, how about I help you work on conquering those anxieties? I promised to give you advance tuition. Why don't you jump in tandem with me?'

'I'm still not sure. Let's not talk about it,' she urged.

Archie Muir popped his head around the door. 'Last orders now, Max. Want anything? Hey, have you seen your photo, by the way? It's all over the newspaper.'

Max and Anya looked up in surprise.

'The *Scottish Recorder*'s here, and you're both in a starring role,' Archie said cheerfully, and presented them with the newspaper.

Max watched with concern as the colour drained from Anya's face.

'You're joking! Please say it's not true.'

She took the paper out of Archie's

hands and hurriedly scanned the piece.

'They've used my address again!' she exclaimed. Her expression was stricken.

'You want to go?' he checked.

She nodded, looking shocked and still staring between him and the newspaper piece.

'Anya, try and stay calm,' he soothed. 'We'll sit down and work out what's the matter.'

'I know what's the matter,' she replied tersely. 'I'm in big trouble because a national paper has printed my private details, putting Callum at risk.'

'Are you OK?' Archie asked uneasily, looking at their faces.

'It's a private matter. Can I keep this?' Max asked, motioning to the paper as he stood up. 'I think we'll head off now. Keep the change, Arch.' He left a clutch of notes on the table to cover the bill.

Anya wasn't merely upset. She was shaking so badly he had to slide his arm around her shoulders to steady her.

Max frowned. She needed to get herself under control if they were going to make any progress in sorting this mess out.

'Listen, I see you're upset but try to calm down.'

She turned on him with slanted eyes and a breaking voice. 'Don't tell me to calm down. Can't you see the extent of the damage this might cause?'

Max took her wrists in his firm grasp. 'Look at me.' He held her blue-grey gaze captive. 'I've been there, remember? I recognise your fear because I've lived it. I hid from a man who beat me witless; I've been on the wrong side of a man with more violent tendencies than brain cells. My dad was probably as bad as your son's. An idiot who didn't deserve to live near human life, let alone parent it. So I understand, and we'll sort this. But you going into traumatised shock isn't going to solve anything. You must stay strong for Callum, because you're in the right. Let me take care of you. How many times do I have to ask that?'

He brushed her hair away from her eyes. 'I know you're frightened, but we'll deal with it together. Let me help you.'

Looking up at him, she said simply, 'Take me home now, Max. Please?'

★ ★ ★

Anya fumbled with the keys in the lock, shaking against the night chills in her thin jacket. Max stood behind her, waiting. All he could think about was her fraught mental state.

'Why don't I get you a drink? Come on, sit down.' He followed her through to the lounge and watched her sit down on the sofa.

'There are bottles in the dresser, help yourself,' she told him blankly. 'I won't have one or I may be sick.'

Max opened the first bottle that came to hand, which happened to be brandy, and poured out a small glassful. 'At least try a sip for the shock.'

He sat beside her and removed her jacket, then handed her a glass. She sipped and grimaced.

Her hair smelled of citrus. Was he getting in too deep?

And yet a tiny whiff of the brandy served to counteract his mood. The sharp tang of alcohol was a smell familiar from his own childhood, the sour breath of booze and bitterness. And it went along with a memory of hands that dealt out blows on a whim.

Glancing around Anya's lounge, taking in Callum's paintings and star charts, Max realised he'd missed out on so much. It all contrasted so starkly with his past. He'd been the kind of kid who could stand up to the toughest bully in the school and never flinch. He got much worse at home. He didn't cry or resist. He took the pain. What were a few licks of a cane when at home you were dished out worse?

Max pushed those ugly thoughts and memories aside. They contrasted too sharply with the homely idyll of Anya's child-friendly cottage.

'Callum's a lucky boy,' Max murmured, looking back at her. 'I know you're upset at the newspaper article and you're probably feeling your anonymity's been jeopardised. But if things do turn nasty, we can always go to the authorities.'

'I'm not turning Callum's life upside down because of my own stupidity!'

'You'll do what has to be done, and we both know it.'

'I'd never have done that photoshoot if I'd thought the story would circulate so widely. I've been so foolish! I'm mad at myself for this. Callum means everything to me. How can I sleep, worrying about what this might bring to our door?'

Max took the glass from her fingers. Their hands brushed, skin on skin, a light touch that sparked between them. Her eyes met his and he didn't break the contact. Her vulnerability sucker-punched him. 'It sounds like Callum's birth parents have plenty in common with mine. Not exactly lifetime members of the good-guy club. But you've no reason to feel guilty here. You can't hide away for the rest of your life.'

She looked at him in direct challenge. Max recognised the glimmer of confusion and courage in the woman. He longed to kiss her, fiercely and meaning every second of it. Make her see he was different, that she should take a chance on him, he'd prove his worth.

Haunted and vulnerable grey-blue eyes made his heart stir into ready life. And fired his emotions in equal measure.

'I should never have been so foolish.'

'He probably doesn't even read newspapers.'

'But what if he does? It's all my fault.'

He stilled her words by pressing his finger against her mouth. It felt great, touching those amazing lips. And somehow the tenor of their discourse was changing. It had started as shared secrets and solemn confessions, but the honesty and the intimacy of their contact changed that. The undeniable chemistry was breaking through.

Max pulled her head against his shoulder. 'We'll get through this, honey. It'll be OK. That's a promise. I won't let anything put Callum's safety at risk.'

Her curves fit his body and made him yearn to move deeper and closer. To inhale the smell of her. The desire to taste her lips burned in his soul.

He yearned to let his hands skim those soft curves. Her body language invited him in. *Did she feel it too?*

'Max, I feel like such a mess, and I don't like you seeing me this way.'

Her gaze flicked to the open neck of his shirt, and he immediately knew she did. He could see in her eyes that she needed this comfort as much as he did.

'You're not a mess. You're mesmerising.' Max reached out to gently trace a line from brow to jaw line on her creamy skin. 'You make it hard for me to concentrate on anything but you. In work time. And everywhere else.'

The firelight blazed and reflected in eyes that communicated longing.

'You must tell me if I'm out of line. I want to hold you and kiss you.'

She whispered softly, 'Maybe I need that too.'

Max pulled her towards him. His mouth met gently hungry lips that welcomed him. He groaned when she moved to wrap her arms around his neck, then pulled him close. It felt like coming home.

He told her, 'I didn't plan on this. You have to believe that.'

'I don't want to be alone tonight. This isn't like me, Max. But would you stay?' She kissed him as she trembled in his arms.

'I shouldn't when you're vulnerable. I should go now.'

'I don't want you to, Max.' She pulled him to her. 'I just want to be held tonight. Sometimes being sensible just means you're hurt and lonely.'

Max kissed her like he'd wanted to. It reminded him of the day he'd first felt a surge of longing at her beauty; muffled above the rim of a scarf at a football match two years before. He knew there was no going back.

'We're both adults. And I don't want to be on my own tonight. That's the honest truth.'

'Then you won't be,' he answered.

10

'Want to talk?' Max's voice was all dark silk and warm promise, laced with a touch of hesitancy. The darkness surrounding them, and the way he lay with her spooned against him, made it easier to speak — they couldn't look into each other's eyes this way.

For a moment, it reminded her of Grant and his *Want to talk?* entreaties of old. Yet there was a world of difference between Grant and Max.

Max desired her; he had some deep-seated impulse to relay his interest and regard. Freakiest of all, he often understood her inclinations without explanation; it felt like he saw her hidden depths and approved.

But had she got it all wrong? Encouraging him to stay so swiftly just wasn't her style, so why be different with this man?

Grant had never inspired her to act so out of character.

Even now she felt the zap of the energy that pulsed between them. Her body fitted his warm male lines. It felt good, but it also felt weird — and, if she were honest, hazardous. Light years away from professional chit-chat across a surgery meeting desk. And straight from the shallows to the deep end without due preparation.

'Last night, I think I moved too swiftly. I really shouldn't have done that. I was upset, I apologise for reaching out to you. It wasn't fair.'

'Anya, we're both grown adults. You needed me. I wanted to stay.'

Anya said simply, 'We do seem to have altered the boundaries now.'

The moonlight spilled across the woollen rug on her bedroom floor. A mauve and aqua rug Grant had bought her as a birthday present. Staring up at her like a bleak reminder by the bed. Was she subconsciously keeping the fortress of her past firmly closed? Or had she just gate-crashed its ramparts by getting close to Max?

Years ago, she'd felt powerless to improve her inability to conceive. Tonight she'd felt the same helplessness in an entirely different way. She felt helpless to resist the man beside her. It was a bittersweet kind of powerlessness she'd never felt before.

'Neither of us planned this. So I'm guessing you're as blown away as me?'

She nodded. 'And guilty.'

'Guilty? We're both single, aren't we? We aren't hurting anyone.'

She was afraid to speak, in case her voice betrayed her spiralling emotions. A raspy catch lying in her throat and tremulous feelings stopped her from voicing them.

'A one-night stand isn't my style,' she whispered.

'I've no regrets.' Max turned onto his side to face her. 'Last night, emotions were high, but it was no mistake. Or a one-night-only deal.' He brushed the hair from her face to see her better.

Anya sighed. 'Will working together be awkward?'

'You should know enough about me already to realise that I'll do my utmost to prevent that. I still want there to be something between us.' Max kissed her tenderly and Anya shivered, serious thoughts taking hold of her mind.

She pulled away, shaking her head. 'I'm not ready for a full-tilt relationship, Max. There's Callum to consider, and we need to take our time, and — '

'And I should go,' Max finished for her. He definitely sounded hurt but there was nothing she wanted to say to negate her statement. She couldn't lie; it would be foolish to pretend they didn't have a lot to get past.

Anya turned to check his expression. Max was watching her with dark eyes.

She seized courage. 'I think it will be best if we cool things and keep it light for now.'

He checked, 'This isn't about the thing with Callum's birth dad, is it?'

She shook her head. 'No. It's been so

sudden, that's all.'

'Can I phone you later?'

'Yes. Just don't push too hard.' She smiled, despite the realisation Max would be sneaking out of her house in the middle of the night, pushing his bike around the corner to avoid detection. *Wasn't that somehow a marker for a cooldown?*

'No regrets,' Max said, half bathed in moonlight, just before he disappeared from her view. A minute later she heard the front door click shut on the floor below. She went down behind him to check he'd posted the key through.

Anya returned to bed, trying her hardest to sleep. All the time, her pulse raced as if she were on a fairground ride on triple speed with no one there to hit the off-switch. Her mind was as full of her own folly as it was of the man who'd ransacked her peace of mind.

As far as any future with Max went, she was closed for business. At heart, she couldn't offer him more without facing up to infertility disappointments again.

11

What had she been thinking? When Anya woke up at past seven the next morning, the implications of the night before sank in fully. Her sheets still bore his lime scent, and the memory of him under those pinky-grey covers huddled close in her memory. And shocked her, too.

Idiot!

'Where was your composure last night?' she asked herself. 'Where was the calm restraint?'

She showered and dressed swiftly, then vigorously brushed her hair in the mirror as if trying to make amends for her lapse through the punishment. She tried to ignore her flushed cheeks. She'd made an error of judgement. She just had to get on and stay sensible. There was no room for Max in her cosy, son-centred lifestyle. There couldn't be. Nothing, repeat *nothing*, could ever be on the cards between her and Dr. Max Calder.

* ★ ★ ★ *

'Hope you don't mind me dropping by?'

Max's boyish smile was dynamite. The oil on his cheek was a killer look.

His presence upended her even though she'd mentally practiced this scene in her head; seeing him again, and acting cool and pragmatic.

Max was on her doorstep in the late afternoon, and Anya was utterly unprepared. Unprepared for him to call round unannounced; for his impact on her senses; for him to upend her equilibrium. Dressed down and scruffy from bike mechanics. A worn-to-thin T-shirt displaying his firm chest.

'I tried to call you but your line was engaged, so I've dropped by from the garage. The bike needed some attention. And so do you. I missed you.'

'Mechanics is dirty work,' Anya answered, flustered.

'I'm good at dirty work.'

In truth, she was looking anywhere but him, trying not to meet his gaze head-on. They needed that chat — the one where she told him to back off properly. He needed to know in no uncertain terms. And it was a ticking time-bomb that made her both nervous and guilty.

'What did you want, Max?'

He stared hard at her as he rubbed his oil-smeared cheek. 'I just wanted to see you. Check all is well. Can I come in?'

Anya pulled the door slightly closed. 'I'm in the middle of making Callum's tea, and Mum's here too. It's awkward.'

She noted the hurt but serious look that took hold at her words. His gaze darkened and narrowed.

'Right. Then I need to say goodbye. What with last night, I never got around to discussing my plans.'

'Goodbye?'

Max shrugged his shoulders. 'I'll be out of the office for the next few weeks. My aunt's had a hip operation, and she needs help, so I volunteered. I won't be at work, and I didn't want you to think I'd fallen down a black hole. Struan okayed the arrangement at interview. My aunt needs a nurse and I'm first in line.'

Anya nodded, inwardly reeling from his surprise news. 'I hope she recovers well soon.'

'And I hope so too . . . You seem distant.' Max's voice had lowered but the concern was clear on his face.

She took a deep breath. 'I think it's the wisest move that we step back. Both of us.'

Max rubbed his chin thoughtfully at her words and scuffed his boots. 'So I shouldn't call you? Is that what you're saying?'

He wasn't making this easy for her. But then, how could she have ever imagined it would be easy? Her feelings for Max Calder weren't simple. 'It's how things have to be for me. I can't get into emotional entanglements.'

He nodded sombrely. 'I'll give you some time and space. Perhaps me being away is for the best, then.'

Max pivoted on long legs and straddled the bike with ease. He pulled on his helmet and started the engine without looking at her.

It kick-started the loud and rattling guilty feelings she'd managed to evade. They rumbled as hard as the engine roared.

Max pulled on thick leather biker gloves, U-turned, and exited her road.

He'd gone. She'd done it.

So why does it hurt?

'Mummy,' called Callum from the lounge, 'I've eaten my vegetables. What's for pudding?'

Callum wasn't the only one who had listened. Only in Max's case she now had to deal with the memory of the look on his face as he'd turned away.

★ ★ ★

Max may only have been at Cala Muir briefly, but strangely his absence was keenly felt once Anya got back to work and he was away on mercy duty for his aunt.

Every time the phone on Anya's desk rang, she found herself privately hoping it was Max. And yet that was the very thing she'd told him to refrain from doing.

She immersed herself in work, but the memories of that night stayed with her. As time passed, she started to suspect this enforced absence was exactly the reprieve she needed. She *had* to get him out of her brain.

As if on cue the phone on her desk rang and Anya picked it up, a part of her flying into a flurry that it could be Max.

'Hello, Anya speaking.'

'I hear Max is away. How's work?' Katie asked.

'Busy,' she answered, omitting any comment about Max.

'Fancy meeting up?' Katie quizzed.

'Can I come over to yours? I wanted to show you the fantastic sponsorship effort and make plans about the jump.'

She'd pushed the jump right back to the backburner of doom in her mind where she had hoped it might fade and die.

'Sure. Say, eightish.' But her heart felt heavy.

Yet it wasn't the time to face up and annoy Katie. She'd hurt Max; she couldn't face having her best friend mad at her too.

Only a matter of minutes later, the phone rang again, and part of her suspected it was Katie. But, of course, it could be Max — and why exactly was she still hoping that?

'Anya Fraser speaking. Can I help you?'

The line was dead. Nope, not dead. The line was open, but no one spoke. A slight crackle gave it away.

'Who's there?' she urged as it clicked off.

Now it was dead. The person had

hung up, leaving her unaware of who it had been. Maybe it had been Katie redialling in error? But surely Katie would have apologised.

She replaced the receiver, feeling as unnerved by the incident as she was disappointed that it hadn't been Max. If he did care for her as much as he'd suggested, why didn't he try getting in touch?

Anya sat staring at the phone. She told herself it had been a wrong number. Phone calls with no one answering were just something that happened. It didn't mean anything sinister, did it? It could be a kid playing a prank. Or someone with nothing better to do, trying to freak her out.

On no account would she let herself even consider it could be Callum's birth father. She had enough worry to wade through. Getting spooked out by phone calls was the last thing she needed.

'Relax, you're making things worse!' she told herself. But the unsettled feelings in her belly still tossed in spite of her attempts to gloss them away. 'Stop seeing ghosts that aren't there.'

*   *   *

Katie had hooked up with her several times during the first week of Max's absence, but Anya had never once admitted to her private date with him. She kept that confidential. Nor did she confess her growing fear about the forthcoming parachute jump, only three weeks away. Her mounting reluctance to participate wasn't something she felt ready to confess, but she was aware time was sprinting on.

Work seemed slow. Everything seemed paler and less interesting minus the presence of the newest senior partner with the friendly banter and lingering smile.

Anya even heard colleagues in the staffroom pining, and had to make an excuse to leave lest she show her edgy feelings.

'I spoke to Max this morning,' Lucy

in reception boasted. 'He said his aunt's feeling a little better, and he's managed to do a spot of fishing.'

Wasn't sitting by the water with a line in hand a touch sedate for the guy who climbed mountains and jumped from huge heights? Maybe she didn't know him at all.

'And Struan has approved an extra week's leave for him because he has some jobs he needs to do, renovating his aunt's home fixtures to assist her. Typical Max. Always has to be busy doing something new! Going the extra mile!' Lucy laughed.

That, Anya could well imagine. But she pulled her thoughts away from dwelling on Max and what he was doing.

He'd only been away for two weeks. Why should that matter? Especially to her. She had made her decision; she had to keep her subconscious in tune with its logic. Max wasn't going to be part of her life.

12

The day before Max was due to return to work after three weeks of leave, Anya's work life was busy. Her final appointment was Vera Brooks, who regularly came into the surgery for blood tests.

Her condition was recently-diagnosed rheumatoid arthritis. This meant she'd been prescribed gold injections, starting with a low dosage because of side-effects. Her rheumatologist was monitoring her blood test results for signs of these.

Anya pulled her seat up and tied the tourniquet around Vera's arm. As she did so, she felt herself grow a touch uncomfortable and clammy.

It wasn't the heat, because she'd already remarked that she felt cold and had hunted out her spare cardigan in her office.

She shook her head and tried to

dispel the feeling.

Maybe she was tired? Maybe she had too much on her mind?

Anya had to concentrate as hard as she could to get through the visit, a fixed grin on her face. But still her fingers shook as she prepared the hypodermic needle, then flicked the vein to make it more pronounced. She felt her breathing quicken and sweat trickle down her back.

She realised she was forcing herself to keep down her stomach contents. By focusing hard, and taking gulps of breath, she managed. The blood was taken and stored as it should be. Then, as soon as Mrs Brooks departed, Anya turned and promptly leant over the tiny sink basin to throw up.

The diligent practice nurse who'd never had a day's sick leave in her entire time at Cala Muir was suddenly unwell.

Perhaps it was just everything she'd had to contend with lately. The silent calls that unnerved her (she'd now had five in total). Her name and address appearing in newspapers; the thought of a parachute jump that terrified her rigid — not to mention her bad feelings about how she'd treated Max. She blamed too much stress on a whirring mind and empty tummy as a recipe for sickness. And reminded herself that often kids carried all sorts of bugs home from nursery.

She stared hard at the sink bowl and dried her mouth with a paper towel. She'd been feeling nauseous on and off all day. Finally, the blood test had pushed her over the edge.

Part of her was shocked she'd thrown up; part of her disgusted. She palmed cool water over her forehead, her thoughts whirling like a confused cyclone. Her eye caught the calendar on the wall, and she remembered that her period should really have arrived by now. And late periods could be due to stress, too.

Anya shook her head, remembering the old days when she'd willed her period *not* to come. With her history, she'd as much chance of pregnancy as she had of joining a medal-winning pro skydiving team. It would no doubt come soon.

She took out the cleaning solution and sponge kept in the drawer nearby, and scrubbed the basin scrupulously.

Thank goodness she had a week off booked in a few days' time. At least she'd be able to calm down. And avoid Max upon his return.

She'd get some rest, and if she was going down with a bug she could get over it and recover. Hopefully she wouldn't pass it on to Callum or her mother. She'd medicate herself and lie low in bed until it passed.

There was a knock on the door. 'Hello, hope you don't mind me dropping by.'

There stood Max. He looked handsome in a trendy suit that did everything for his frame.

'I hope you've had a good rest while I've been away.' He looked chastened.

'Hardly. It's been pretty busy here. I

hope your aunt is well.

'Much improved.' His gaze darted away. 'It's a work-related call. I was letting everyone know I'm back, seeing if there's any emergencies or problems.'

Anya realised if he'd been half a minute quicker and had caught her throwing up, she'd have died!

His hair was dark and appealing. If she'd played things differently the day he'd left, he'd be coming over right now to plant a kiss on her mouth. Now all Anya could do was grip the sink and wish. Hopefully the lemony smell of the sink cleaner covered up her sins.

'I'm fine.'

'You don't look yourself, Anya. You look pale.'

'Just tired. Truly.'

So *fine* that the lemon smell of sink cleaner was making her insides churn again. Her knees wobbled and she tried her hardest not to let herself retch.

'Still firm about us being off-limits, even after the space?' he asked softly. She felt his gaze rove over her as if storing her up. 'What are you doing tonight? We could talk. But there's no pressure.'

'I may have to delay that, as I think I may have a bug coming on. Sickness, and I'm a touch dizzy too.' A fresh wave of dizziness was taking hold. She gripped the sink and vowed to stand and weather it. 'And anyway, I still think distance is best between us.'

He watched intently, concern in his eyes, then walked towards her in long strides to palm her forehead. 'You don't feel like you're running a temperature, but you look washed out. Want to go home?'

'I've patients to see. I'll get through it.'

'No. Home you go. I'll take you,' he said commandingly. 'Have you been eating, sleeping?'

'Ish.'

'Let me go and talk to Struan. I'll come back for you in five minutes. Get your things,' he instructed her.

Anya tried her best to smile before he

left, to prove she could do it and he was overreacting. She did look tired, she did look pale; she could see her reflection. She also felt terrible. *But is it really just a bug? Surely eight years without a positive pregnancy isn't going to be changed by one night with Max? It had been impulsive, but we'd taken care . . . had it somehow gone wrong?*

Her hand went to her stomach, and then she forced her thoughts away.

'Thank goodness I'm off for a week's leave,' Anya told herself. 'Jittery, acting jumpy and out of character . . . I need a rest!'

The phone rang on her desk, but as soon as she answered, it clicked off.

She'd been getting these anonymous calls all week now. It spooked her so silly she couldn't think straight. Someone was either trying to frighten her — and doing a great job of it — or she was getting things all out of proportion and the practice needed an engineer to come out and fix the telephone system.

But if she was getting crank calls and

it was the person she suspected, it was the one thing she'd dreaded since Callum had come into her life all those months ago. The abusive father she'd worked so hard to keep away from him — the direst of dads. If he was trying to scare her, no doubt he'd soon make a move. He knew where she worked and he knew where she lived. He probably even knew where Callum went to nursery. Fear speared Anya at the thought. He could be biding his time until he made some demand.

Anya, fist knotted on the receiver, shoved the phone back into its cradle with a smack.

'Callum's mine now,' she whispered. 'I won't let you scare me!'

Five seconds later, her knees buckled beneath her and she fell into a faint.

* * *

'Don't make such an almighty fuss. One little fainting episode. Hardly life-threatening!' Anya protested.

Max felt his jaw tense as he stared down at her, his mind racing. He probably looked like a riled Viking warrior with hands on hips, glowering like thunder at the woman. But he couldn't hide his frustration at Anya's dismissive attitude. She was lying on her bed in her cottage, and Max was having no truck with her excuses.

'Be quiet and be a good patient, eh?' He wished she'd stop the Miss Independent act. It frustrated him because it felt like a barricade to ward off all challenges. To shoot down all his attempts to get close to her.

She pouted. 'Do I have a choice?'

'You could have had a nasty gash there — you missed the corner of the filing cabinet by inches. And you knocked your head on the floor. I'm just suggesting it's time for some recuperation.'

'But I'm fine.'

'And I'm the doctor. Your mother is taking care of your son. You're due for a week's leave in two days' time. So don't come back to work until after your break. Rested, recuperated, and ready to serve.'

Truth be told, her fainting episode had scared him sideways. The panic that had caught in his chest and sent him whirring into fight-or-flight had stunned even him. And told him in no uncertain terms that Anya Fraser mattered to him. It served to make him wonder if this was the kind of home-and-heart woman Aunt Vi had talked of.

Anya affected him deeply. That in itself was scary.

But it wasn't like her to keel over, and he wondered what had caused this. He could see the strain marks around her eyes. Was there something she wasn't telling him? Was she still worrying about the jump? Was that what had brought this on?

Max scanned the thermometer. 'Your temperature's fine. Everything seems normal. Feeling dizzy . . . woozy . . . anything?'

'I'm OK. I did skip lunch, though. But that's hardly something new.'

'Skipping lunch shouldn't result in a fainting reaction, Anya. Does 'skipping lunch' translate as missing more meals than you're letting on? Don't tell me you're dieting.'

'No diets, I love my food too much. I had breakfast. Don't nag. I'll be fine in a minute.'

She pulled herself up on the bed to a sitting position.

Max shook his head at her. 'You're going nowhere.' Gently, he pressed her back onto the bed. 'There's only one thing for it. I'm putting your mum on security duty!'

'That's a prison sentence.'

He watched her lying there, and itched to take care of her all by himself.

'Got any windows on your week off? Any chance I could take you and Callum for lunch?'

He'd heard what she'd said earlier about distance. He'd gone over that conversation they'd had about 'space' often enough in his head all the time he'd been away in Ardfoyle. Seeing her again made his resolve crash and burn. He still wanted more. He needed another chance, a shot at making her see he was worth it.

She shook her head.

In seconds, before reasoned thoughts could dissuade him, his lips sought hers. She was clearly surprised, but she responded after several seconds. He groaned softly against her skin. She tasted fantastic and had him yearning for more . . . to touch, explore, enjoy.

'You've no idea how I've gone over and over this in my mind. It's made me crazy.'

She might be evading him with words, claiming a need for space. But one kiss had demonstrated how much their chemistry transcended that. He'd missed her, and she felt the same. It moved her as deeply as it did him. They were both shaking with the power of it.

'Why do you keep pushing me? Why

won't you listen?' she begged him in a whisper.

He pushed her hair away from her face and stared into those amazing eyes.

'Do I seem like the guy who takes a few nos for an answer?' he asked softly. 'Who wants distance when we can share this?'

'But it can't be anything more.'

'We have now, why overanalyse? Why not take this for what it is?'

His lips traced a line from her brow to her cheek. It would have been so easy to kiss her passionately again. Only the knowledge that her mother was downstairs, playing with modelling clay with young Callum, might have dampened his ardour.

'You're irresistible.'

She rolled sassy eyes. 'I've been sick. Hardly nice.'

Max's posture stiffened as she averted her gaze to a floral embroidery patch on the coverlet. 'You were sick? You never said. Could you have a virus?'

In a blink, she hitched herself straighter and hugged those bedclothes firm. Evading her own faux pas.

'I'm not sure. Probably a little tummy thing, that's all, don't sweat it.'

Max took her hand and kissed it. 'What am I to do with you, Fraser?' he asked. 'You're trouble. And you tell untruths.'

'And you're not trouble?' she whispered back huskily.

He smiled. 'Now, get some rest, and I'll keep my distance until you're fit. You're no good to me fainting and swooning. But I intend to fix a lunch date. No taking no for an answer.'

'Doctor's orders?'

'Most definitely. So don't argue.' Slowly, he walked out of the room.

With a glint in her eye, she softly remarked, 'Now I see what you're like with your patients. Attentive but forceful, Dr. Calder.'

13

Max was as good as his word. He stayed away and decreed that Anya should take an enforced break to get back to full fitness. So she took his advice and rested up.

Her mother looked after Callum and she ate well, slept in, drank tea and read books. She even looked through some magazines; an unheard-of achievement since Callum's arrival. And she worked on calming herself and introducing some reasoned logic to her prior concerns about the anonymous phone calls at work.

Why should she assume it was Callum's birth dad frightening her on purpose? What other evidence supported that conclusion? Nothing. It was simply her own anxiety about the front-page picture.

In the sanctuary of her bedroom,

reading her novel and sipping chamomile tea, she could see she was overreacting. The anonymous calls were most likely coincidence. Maybe a prankster with little sense or sensitivity for the implications of their actions? She could tell Max casually about them so the practice could monitor how calls were handled in future.

She'd needed these days off to gather her reserves, to de-stress and take stock. And, to be honest, the rest was doing her good. She hadn't fainted. She hadn't felt quite so sick. She'd been grazing on her meals, and it seemed to have settled her constitution better.

Things were looking up, and she'd kept Thursday aside for lunch.

Anya picked up the telephone on her bedside table and dialled. When Max answered his desk phone at work, she smiled.

'I'm feeling much better, Doctor Calder. You mentioned lunch?'

'You sound chirpy, and I'm pleased to hear it.'

'So, where are we going for this mystery lunch date? Callum can't wait.'

Max gave a response she could tell was a cover-up because he must be with a patient.

'That will be no trouble, leave it with me. I'll get right back to you.'

She chuckled as she replaced the receiver. Things were definitely looking up. Amazing what a few days off work could achieve. Maybe Max's orders had merit?

* * *

When Max called round at eleven-thirty on Thursday, she feigned cheery composure. Surely they could be friends . . . and Max had been right. They did get on really well; he was good with Callum; so why not enjoy the present? They could take things slow, and see how it went. Why did she have to blight the bond between them so suddenly? If he was prepared to be patient, maybe they could have a future of sorts.

'After lunch, I want to take you and Callum out for a very special treat,' he announced. She could hear the smile in his voice and couldn't help wondering what he was hatching. 'What's your answer?'

'Depends on where you want to take us.'

'Somewhere Callum will love to go, trust me. You OK?'

'I'm fine. So where, Max?'

'Somewhere you can experience the first step towards skydiving.' She could hear the amusement in his voice.

The thought made her doubts swirl. 'Can't we forget that for now? Hasn't it already got me into enough trouble?'

'I know the superintendent at Abershiel Fire Station. He's offering Callum the run of the place for fun. And, if you're good, he'll let me take you up the tower to conquer this heights aversion.'

'No way.' Suddenly her stomach was doing panic somersaults.

'Yes! I intend to familiarise you

gently with the task in hand. Have you ever been up a fire station tower before? It'll be the perfect first step. Then I plan to take you up the fire engine ladder. It's a great plan, plus I'll be there to talk you through it.'

She raked a hand through her hair. 'Are you crazy? I can't do it.'

'You can and you will,' he told her. 'Remember, I'll be there helping you all the way.'

'You'd better bring a sick bag along, then.'

'You'll be fine. I'll hold your hand. And I've got a special friend in the fire service who might even let Callum go in the engine for fun if his mum's a good girl and does as she's told.'

'Don't make me do this. Bribery won't work either.'

'Trust me, I'm a medical professional. I wouldn't stoop to bribing you, but by the end of today you'll be a step closer to achieving your goal.' That was the thing about daredevils. They had the utmost conviction in their beliefs.

He was so good for her, it caused an ache in her soul. It would take her mind off things — and her son would love it. A chance to see real firefighters in action, and sit in a big red engine, and wear a fireman's hat. He'd love Max to bits for ever after; how could she possibly say no?

Especially when she was one hundred and fifty-nine percent smitten. Falling, precarious because of how he made her feel, melting from the toenails up with his every word and smile. This man was getting inside places she'd long sealed over for protection.

'Just don't expect too much of me,' she quipped.

Max's voice had dulcet tones that persuaded. 'Why would I do that? I know what you're capable of, and I'm already impressed beyond words.'

✱   ✱   ✱

'Relax; everything's going to be fine.'

Anya winced. The wall of the tower

was at her back, and she was keeping herself welded to it like a rusty rivet on an old bridge, stuck with an amalgam mix of superglue and abject fear.

'Come here. There's a parapet, you won't fall over. Trust me.'

She gasped. 'I'm shaking inside my underwear. My knees are like barely-set jelly.'

His smile could have tempted anyone to do almost anything.

Max had taken her and Callum along to the local fire station tower. She'd watched the raw joy and delight on her son's face when Max placed him inside a real red engine, his excitement so palpable he nearly burst. Callum was as excited to meet several real-life fire-fighters in the flesh, too. Especially when they showed him the hose used to extinguish blazes. She watched his little mouth fall wide open in awe.

'He can't take it all in!' she exclaimed.

'He'll remember this for the rest of his life. Boys love fire engines. I know that I did,' Max confessed. 'Reggie, show this young man around the station and give him access to a fireman's hat, please.'

'Right-oh, Doc,' said burly Reggie Marshall with a wicked wink and a faux salute. 'Fancy another sit inside the cabin? This time behind the wheel, once we've got your helmet on?' Callum couldn't nod fast enough.

And now he was a tiny speck below that she could hardly bring herself to look down on. Anya forced herself to stand beside Max at the ledge of the tower.

'It's high.'

'Wave to Callum, now, he's watching,' he instructed.

She did in spite of wobbling legs.

'See, it's not so bad, is it? Max slipped his arm deftly around her waist.

Not so bad! It's terrifying. Just like I'm feeling with you. I'd vowed to resist, to hold strong, to keep Callum my priority, and you're sneaking through my emotional perimeter fence.

What am I going to do when you ask about tomorrows I can't give?

How will you react when I ask you to give up risk-taking because I can't handle the consequences?

She looked at him with shock, fear and utter trepidation. 'It's worse than terrifying. But I've no choice. I have to do this jump. Max, you have to help me.'

'And I am. They're going to raise you and me back up here on the engine ladder — think you can handle that?'

'No.' She squeezed her eyes shut. She wished her pulse wasn't racing. Wished her heart wasn't doing what felt like crazy Grand Prix speed circuits. Wished she had the oomph and bravado to take all this in her stride and not look like a total ninny in front of Max.

Twenty minutes later she was doing it. Her legs had wobbled like crazy, but she'd clung to Max and suffered it. She'd gone up the ladder and even waved to Callum, grimace-faced and all. When they reached the ground again, he turned her to face him.

'You did it. You'll do the jump. You can go in tandem with me. I have faith you'll do it.'

'I think you're crazy, and I must be too.'

Crazy to let myself fall under your spell. Crazy to risk my heart all over again.

'Crazy about you.' He pressed a warm, citrus-smelling kiss into her hair. She revelled in the touch; it almost made the knee wobbliness go away of its own accord.

'Don't, Max! Don't make this hard.'

'It already is hard.' The nerves in his cheeks tightened and he looked sombre suddenly. 'I had a letter arrive while I was away at my aunt's. A job I went for ages ago, before I came to Cala Muir. For the Crisis Medicine Agency in Turin. They've offered me a position. A mega job. The kind I used to dream about. I'm amazed I've been offered it, in fact, and it's hard to turn down.'

The guy took her up forty-odd feet in

the air, then sprung this kind of surprise and expected her to stay vertical! Was he joking? She felt her knees wobble.

'I'm not going to take it.' His face played a mix of emotions. 'I think we have something special, and while it's early days, I don't want to walk away. But what I guess I'm saying is, I hope we could have a future worth staying for. I'm saying you're my priority. Don't push me away.'

Her thoughts scuffled inside her brain and created a ruckus she couldn't decipher. 'It's way too soon. If it's your dream job, you should take it. You shouldn't turn such a thing down because of me.'

He looked instantly abashed.

'Don't just dismiss us like that.'

'I told you when we first got to know each other. I can't offer futures. Why won't you get that?'

'Because I care. Because I hoped you'd see past it and realise what we share is special.'

Anya's face grew taut with frustration. 'You're running ahead way too fast. Crazy speed. I'm sorry, but I can't go inventing fairy-tale endings for this.'

It reminded her of Grant. Always pushing, never listening; it pressed all her angry buttons at once. With Grant, she'd tried to make him see her view, but he'd had an irritating and overbearing tendency to run ahead of himself and often go over her head. Like with the promotion, going behind her back. Like dismissing adoption out of hand.

Would Dr. Max Calder treat her exactly the same? Deciding she was his future, and ignoring all her warnings for caution? If so, now was the time to hold up a placard that said 'stop'.

He whispered, 'I'm falling for you. I can't help that. And that scares me more than heights do you.'

'I wouldn't count on it,' she said. Her legs were shaking so hard she had to grab onto him. 'You're pushing me way further than I want to go, Max. I can't give you promises yet, so don't ask for them.'

Her legs were still far from steady. Whether it was the ladder experience or the revelation from the man, she wasn't sure.

Callum ran towards them, waving like crazy and grinning from ear to ear. The smallest, cutest, best-looking mini-fireman she'd ever seen in her life. It filled her heart to bursting — or it would have, had her stomach not been in a million vertigo-challenged knots.

She loved Callum so very much. She was lucky to have him, and she'd thought her heart was only big enough for one all-consuming love like that. But now there was Max, and he pulled it in other directions. Only Anya wasn't sure that the two could go comfortably together. He thrived on danger, on making her confront things, taking challenges head-on. And now he was a man who'd make a mark in Turin, Italy.

Had she the right to stop those kinds of dreams?

And what sort of mess was she in now she'd fallen so hard in love with him it knotted her insides up just recognising it? That fact was so frightening, so hard to get her head around, it hurt like an ache.

Max didn't even realise yet he was kidding himself.

She'd seen it with Grant. Max could no more settle for a quiet backwater life in Alderwick for the rest of his days than Grant could have settled for being the village's rural policeman. Sooner or later, he'd resent what he'd given up and seek pastures new. Ultimately their paths would have to go on separate tangents.

She'd been there before. She knew the story by heart. Grant had left her. Max would too. He had too much potential for her to let him waste it.

Anya shook her head. 'I still can't promise you what you want. Callum needs me more. And it's important you reach your career potential. You won't do that at Cala Muir.'

'Trust me, I want us to work,' he urged her. 'I won't let you down.'

'Don't ask me to take the focus away from my son. Don't take the focus off your own life for me.'

Max rubbed his forehead with his palm. 'You're so frustrating; you just won't let me through.'

Anya summarised their prior discussions for him. 'I can't let this turn into a relationship. I have a duty to protect Callum and make him my first priority, always. You should take the job. I can't offer you the future you need.'

'Can't? Or won't?' he asked.

When they jumped down from the engine, he strode off to whirl her son in his arms and round off their visit with feigned bravado. She followed after them, her legs still unsteady even though she was back on solid ground.

14

Max stayed quiet all the way back to her cottage.

He listened to the innocent banter Anya shared with her son: Callum's unfettered excitement about the fire station visit and his jubilant exclamations about how much he'd loved every minute.

But Max's mind was elsewhere.

As soon as he got the chance and Callum was settled with a snack in front of his favourite kids' TV show, Max drew Anya aside into the kitchen.

'Talk to me.'

She shook her head. 'We have to step away from this. It won't work. No matter how hard you push, my mind's made up.'

'What do you mean it won't work? Isn't that a touch premature?'

'You don't want long term and I

don't want a relationship. Doesn't sound like a practical future to me. And this opportunity in Italy is way too good to turn down.'

'Shouldn't I be the judge of that?' he corrected. He paced the kitchen tiles in frustration. 'Maybe I've been too scared to try before. Why are you pushing me away all the time? Suddenly Italy's not so attractive now I've met someone who means so much to me.'

'There's a hard truth I can't get around, and that is that I can't have children. Ultimately, things usually come back to family in the end, and I don't want to go there again. Falling in love with someone eventually turns to thoughts of kids. I can't ever go through that again. It's caused me too much hurt. My life revolves around Callum now. I've made the best of things, and that's how it has to be. I enjoy being with you, we have good times; but I refuse to be railroaded into a future.'

Her words churned inside him.

It was ridiculous. God knew he felt for her and what she'd been through. Infertility was such a huge loss and grief in anyone's life. It ate away and undermined so many things. But Anya was young and vibrant, so why was she writing him off because of her past?

Why won't she trust?

'If I can get through my past, you can surmount yours,' he challenged. 'It doesn't mean you stop living.'

'And what about when you go back to jumping out of planes and climbing sheer faces to get your kicks?'

'What makes you an expert on what I want? I want you. At least give me a chance to prove it.'

'What if I ask you to give up the risk-taking? What if I tell you I can't handle it and Callum needs a safe daddy? What then?'

She was staring hard. He had a hunch she'd got to the nub of one of her major gripes. Why had she never brought this up before?

'You have a problem with me

parachuting, climbing? You want me to stop?'

'I'm saying we're too different. I know you can't stop your outdoor daredevil stuff, because you love it. But slow and safe is my nature, I can't change.'

'I can't promise you I can change. Being an outdoor guy is part of me. I can't stop being who I am.'

She shook her head at him. 'We aren't such a perfect match, are we? And I know you don't want marriage. You evade questions about it and act like talking about it would hurt you. Why would I risk my son's stability when you don't trust me with the truth?'

'Maybe I can't trust anyone with that,' he said darkly.

The truth.

The dark thoughts he pushed to the furthest corner of his mind.

Was that how far he had to go with this woman — to make her see how much she meant?

Max narrowed his eyes.

'You want my truth now? Is that what it will take to convince you?'

'I'm only saying I don't know enough about you to run headlong into some messy affair. You're my boss. Let's leave it at that. Let's stop now before things get any more tangled.'

He pulled her to face him, and his eyes were as bright as they were fiercely solemn. 'I'm already tangled. I'm falling faster and faster; and believe me, it's the last thing I need. I vowed I'd never fall for any woman. My mum and dad's dysfunctional marriage and mutual sense of loathing put me off relationships for life. But you've got me where it hurts most. This is real, it matters, and all I can think of is you. Why don't you get that?'

Still her protests came and his frustration rose. 'With this much baggage it can't work!'

'Why can't we enjoy what we have?'

'Because neither of us can give more.'

Max raked a hand through his hair.

'The reason I was fostered by my aunt was that my dad almost killed me. He was punishing me as the conclusion to a beating. He shut me in the shed at the bottom of the garden. Only he didn't count on me being scared as well as resourceful, and finding matches. The shed was ablaze by the time I escaped. My mother was so incensed she tried to kill my father. She failed, luckily, or there would be a murder charge to add to the sorry picture of my past. The police were called in to sort it out — as were Social Services. The years of beatings came out. Now you know the truth, it makes pretty dark entertainment. And it's not something I care to revisit. So yes, maybe permanent futures aren't something I treat lightly. But I have my reasons.'

She stayed silent, barely meeting his gaze. He turned away, feeling strained; the words had poured out, but even Max had heard the vitriol and pain in his own voice. The past hurt: it always would.

'Oh, Max!' She leant over to touch him and he edged back. 'I didn't mean for you to tell me all that.'

'Don't! It's hard enough to open up without kindness and soft touches. There's very little soft and tender about my baggage.'

'I appreciate you telling me, but it can't change how I feel.'

'Well, I'm alerting you that you're shutting yourself in an emotional bunker. I'm handing you a box of matches. Use them, let yourself get out, find some freedom. Light up your dark corner. Or you'll wind up with a grown-up son, wondering where your life went.'

Twenty seconds later Max had pulled on his jacket, kissed her son goodnight on top of his golden blond head, and gone.

* * *

Anya couldn't stop thinking about Max's revelation.

All week, their exchanges were brief and terse. It was clear he'd washed his hands of trying to talk her round. Or maybe he resented that the exchange in her kitchen had had to happen?

Every night in bed she thought of him. And it wasn't dreaming of Max's attributes. It was Max the child. Locked in a dark space, frightened half to death of the beating to follow at his father's callous hands. Was it any wonder he had a wild streak that drove him up mountains and into planes? Didn't he deserve an outlet for that pent-up emotion?

She'd been wrong.

She might still hold firm to her conviction that a relationship wouldn't be helpful right now. But that didn't mean she couldn't still apologise and build bridges with a man she respected as a friend, did it?

* * *

Lynette was talking with Abi in the practice staffroom. Anya hadn't meant

224

to eavesdrop. She'd been searching through the resources library, crouching on the floor at the back of the room, rummaging for a textbook, and clearly her colleagues hadn't realised she was there.

Lynette said softly, 'Keep this to yourself, but Max has told Struan he's interested in a job in Italy. They want him to go back and see them, and Struan's given him time off. It'll be such a shame if he goes.'

She heard Abi's intake of breath, and felt her own breathing wobble.

'Oh no! Max is such an asset and he's only just got here. He'd be sorely missed.'

'I know, but it's a really high-flying job,' Lynette explained; it seemed she had the inside word on Max's career intentions and views on life. Or maybe the grapevine was more thorough than Anya had ever imagined. 'Apparently he went for it before he took this one. It's a wonderful opportunity. Even Struan agrees he shouldn't dismiss it.'

Anya's hand stilled as she found the book she was looking for, but she didn't have the heart to stand up and reveal herself. Her heart was thundering hard in her chest. Too late, though — she too was about to be dragged into social gossip.

'What about Anya? Does she know?'

'I hear she does. I thought they were getting serious . . . have you seen the way he looks at her? Like something out of some passionate epic film?'

They both made wistful noises that made her suspect she'd been looking at Max like some doe-eyed puppy with a hankering for a new master.

Anya winced. So much for keeping things hush-hush and private. So much for professionalism.

'She'll be devastated. Poor girl's had so many problems. Her partner was killed, and now this. She hasn't had much luck in the relationship department,' Abi opined.

'I'm worried about her. She's not been herself lately. She looks pale.'

'I'd noticed that too.'

'Just goes to show, you never know what's around the corner. Seize life while it's there. Max Calder is perfect partner material, who'd want to pass up that? She should take care or she'll lose him.'

'She's been burned by her past. But he's a good guy at heart.'

She heard her colleagues rinse their coffee mugs and leave the staffroom. She left it a minute before getting back to her feet, colour visible in her cheeks as she passed the wall mirror. Max Calder was going to Italy; she'd told him to go herself. She'd encouraged him, and stated it was a chance he had to take. So she'd have to come to terms with his departure because it would most likely happen. And she'd been the one responsible for pushing him there hardest.

So why was her heart hurting so hard, realising what was going to happen?

★   ★   ★

Max looked up from his case notes, his thoughts disturbed by a soft knock at the door.

'Come in.'

The office door opened, and the door of his heart swung wide with it.

His favourite nurse looked antsy and sombre, and he itched to jump over the desk and pull her into a body-melting hug.

'Please come and have a seat. How can I help?'

'I need to apologise for upsetting you last week. You took me out, you made my son feel special, and all you got for your trouble was me being dismissive.'

He smiled. 'It doesn't matter.'

Max examined her. She looked amazing. He'd missed watching those lips. Even passing her in the corridor and trying to stay immune — smelling her familiar shower-fresh scent — had him virtually crawling the walls not to jump in front of her.

He could barely think straight. The

last week had been utter torment. His patients must be christening him 'the miserable medic'. The daredevil tag was outdated; he'd been grumbling and growling all over the shop.

'I'm sorry; do you accept my apology?'

'Of course.'

'So will you speak to me? I hate seeing you at work and feeling like there's an icy wedge of awkwardness between us. You're a good friend, Max. Both Callum and I have grown very fond of you, and if you go to Italy I want it to be with goodwill.'

A death knell sounded in his heart.

Fond. A very good friend.

'Of course, I'll always speak to you.'

'Even at football last Saturday. I felt as if I'd become invisible or I'd hurt you.'

'I can't lie and pretend it's OK you're turning me down. But I shouldn't ever ignore you. So now it's my turn to apologise.'

She'd rumbled him so well, he felt

utterly foolish at his schoolboy immaturity. She'd looked so gorgeous, and been chatting so animatedly with local flirtation-famed boys Duncan McHugh and Gregor Buchan, that ignoring her was his only means of defence. Punching two guys' lights out in the middle of a public football match wasn't good conduct from a local GP.

'Sorry.' He shrugged his broad shoulders. 'Friends?'

'More than friends,' she amended with a smile. 'The jump is on Saturday. Are you still happy to be my tandem parachute buddy? Or have you gone and got someone else?'

'You're still up for it?' he checked. 'You don't have to do it if it still scares you silly. You were shaking like a leaf up that tower at the fire station.'

'You bet I'm up for it. I've a reputation to maintain. Sponsorship money to honour. A son to keep on side. Whether you want me or not, you've got me, daredevil doctor. I'm going to jump, Max. I've got to.'

'Righto!' he said, amazed at her tenacity and guts. 'We're scheduled for twelve noon on Saturday at Shoresden Airstrip. Turn up, and I'll take you down in tandem and give you the ride of your life.'

Max could read in her body language that she knew she'd altered, perhaps tarnished, their prior friendship.

'I'll be there,' she agreed. Anya Fraser was a woman of her word. Which was a shame. Because she'd resolutely told him they had no future unless it was only as friends.

* * *

All the way to the airfield, Callum was in a state of high excitement. He chattered away with Marion Fraser nineteen to the dozen, and Marion answered with patience and interest — all the time giving her crazy skydiving daughter sidelong looks that told her Marion still truly believed she might be misguided and mad.

'Mum, you're doing it again!'

'What?'

'That look. Stop it — I'm doing this, I can't let them down.'

'Whatever you say, darling.'

'Mummy, Mummy! Will you wave at me when you jump out and give me a thumbs-up?' Cal asked, almost causing Anya to do a U-turn in the road and head for home at eighty miles an hour.

'I will, sweetie. If you're extra good.'

By the time they reached Shoresden, she realised that if Callum was on a high, Katie was frenetic with excited nerves too. Maybe a state of euphoria was her friend's coping mechanism for all-consuming terror?

Within minutes of arriving at the airstrip she had to get herself ready. The Parachuting Practice Nurse pulled on her aviator overalls and fastened herself into her harness with shaky fingers but a determined gritting of her teeth.

She'd do this if it killed her. It might just succeed in that, too. But she'd have Max with her every single millimetre of the way down. Surely that made this bitter pill an easier one to swallow?

Anya looked around and took in the big scary aircraft sitting on the runway. And the gorgeous guy next to it with the amazing physique just had to be Max.

He turned then, and smiled.

She smiled too, and watched as her tiny son shouted, 'Max, it's me — Callum! Can I come and see the cockpit?' He ran like a blond-headed bullet, and was immediately whirled around in Max's arms. It touched the edges of her sensitised heartstrings. And then she noted the video camcorder that was being shoved in her face every two seconds. Until that point she'd been swatting it away like an irritating buzzing insect.

'We're taking a video for Adoption Support Scotland. It might even get included in a training video for adopters,' Katie enthused. 'Won't that be great?'

'Great!' she replied on autopilot.

'Why not say a piece to camera?'

Anya grimaced. 'I'm terrified. Why am I doing this? Why am I putting my heart through the strain? Why?'

'Because you're an amazing woman with a great attitude to life. And you're prepared to make a difference,' a male voice said at her elbow.

Who else but Dr. Calder?

She turned, momentarily blinded by Max's sun-taming grin.

'Prepared?'

'No,' she admitted. '*Petrified* sums it up better.'

'There's no backing out now, honey. It's going to happen, and you'll be right beside me all the way.'

'It's a long way down.'

'You'll revel in every second. Look at that sunshine. The view will be sensational up there.'

Anya didn't give a fig about the view. She'd certainly revel in every second of close proximity to her instructor. She loved the feel of him next to her: his confidence, his assuredness. His *joie de vivre* and rebellious streak that turned her into hormone-jangling mush.

Five minutes later, they were climbing into the aircraft, and Callum was jiggling on the spot, shouting, 'I love you, I love you much, Mummy. *I love you much!*'

The phrase that left her in tearful tatters — the same as Callum's first ever time calling her Mummy. He'd said '*I love you much, Mummy*' and she'd cried all night, half in joy, and half in aching maternal love that caused the dams of relief and past disappointments to flood.

'Love you too, honey. See you soon!' she shouted, keeping her emotions in check.

How could she possibly back out now?

15

Katie's manner changed from euphoria to silence once they were aloft and ascending.

The excitement stilled, and a more serious vein took hold. They were on their way up and there was only one way down.

Max tried to lift the mood, feigning a pilot-style cabin voiceover. 'And if you'd care to look to your left you may just catch a glimpse of Cala Muir Medical Centre — the best medical practice in the land. Enjoy a pleasant stay and we hope to welcome you aboard again soon.'

No one laughed. They were too sick to their stomachs to muster even a giggle of appreciation.

Anya hated every single solitary moment of this. Sweat trickled down her back. Her palms grew clammy and her tongue dried. Then she felt a repeat wave of the sickness. She could have thrown up, but she willed herself not to. At that moment, she realised her period still hadn't arrived.

How could she possibly risk throwing herself out of an aircraft in her current state of mind; stricken silly with fear?

Anya let herself find excuses because she was double figures feet high up in an aircraft about to do a skydive she'd never want to do in the first place. *What if my period is late for a reason? What if I am pregnant — what then?*

She'd been so intent on evading her recent physical symptoms that she hadn't stopped to really analyse what they could mean. The realisation shocked her to the core: the one thing she'd always wanted with all her heart and soul could be true.

Still she'd had no period, but had a sick feeling in her belly and an inability to get this odd metal taste out of her mouth, and here she was about to throw herself bodily into the sky and hurtle through mid-air.

She knew only too well from her day job that mistakes happened. Would she risk such a precious thing through a foolhardy act?

In moments Max was beside her. She stalled before reaching out to him.

'Max . . . '

He raised his eyebrows questioningly and smiled encouragement. 'Don't worry. It'll be plain sailing. I'm here doing it too.'

'I can't do it, Max. Don't make me.'

'C'mon, this is just stage fright, honey. You'll be fine.' His face creased with placation and care.

'I'm serious. I'm backing out now. I should never have come this far.'

He stilled her with his hand and pushed his finger to her lips. 'Katie and Mike are going first. Then Tina and Chris, and we'll go last. You're just nervous; it's natural.'

Anya bit back a scream. No way was she doing the jump with her current doubts and questions unanswered, while she could well be carrying his child.

Katie looked ashen now, but she forced herself on. She made a sterling effort, throwing out a big wide thumbs-up, before she leapt out with her tandem instructor.

Too soon, the plane was empty but for Anya and Max.

'What's the prognosis?' he asked her. 'Still a no?'

'I can't do this. Seriously, believe me. I was foolish to try.'

'You gave it a good shot. Given your history with heights, that was pretty brave.'

Anya felt far from brave, just shell-shocked. 'I should never have gone this far with it. But I can't go any further!' She shook her head.

'I'll never make you do something you don't want to. I've never made you do anything against your will, I couldn't.'

'Don't ask why,' she pleaded. 'Please.'

'I don't need to ask. You're shaking.

You look like you're about to pass out. I don't want you to jump in this condition. I'll check you over when you land. I'm going to jump alone.'

Max stood on the edge before turning to wave, then seconds later he took a step into empty air and clouds.

Anya gasped, even though she knew so well he had more experience at parachuting than most. She still found herself praying for his safety.

Max was going solo. In triumphant daredevil style. And she had let them down for the plain and simple reason that she might be pregnant.

* * *

It was as if the others felt worse for Anya not jumping than she did. Katie was ecstatic and elated at the jump. In fact, her refusal put a slight downer on everyone — not because of the sponsorship element, but because she looked so downcast when the plane got back to terra firma. Anya walked away slowly, feeling sheepish.

'It's OK, Mummy,' said Callum. 'I think you were very brave going up in the plane.'

She kissed his head and bit back the tears.

Max was beside her in moments. That was when she found the tears hardest to keep in check. He'd jumped in front of her, and she'd felt the whirring emotions clog and spin. She loved him. She really cared. Him jumping from a plane in front of her eyes had left her sobbing into her hands.

The parachute jump had clearly demonstrated that Anya was a different breed. Unlike Max, she cowered in the face of adrenaline kicks and dangerous exploits. Why had she ever tried to think differently — and why was she laying her life vulnerable to a man who was built that way and could never change?

Grant had taught her a valuable lesson.

She couldn't handle a risk-taking

man in her life. Her failed charity jump had only helped to clarify that Max Calder really was no different.

'Hey,' said Max, sliding his arm around her shoulders. 'Don't stress. You tried, that's what counts, honey. I'm proud of you.'

He placed a tender kiss in her hair. One that felt like it burned. So many tussling emotions were jostling inside her: thoughts about pregnancy; Max having already won her heart, but her being unable to live with him. It was too much to cope with right now.

'I'm going back up,' he said, clipping himself into his harness. She could see he now had another parachute on his back.

'What are you doing that for?'

'I'll do your jump for you. Salvage some of the sponsorship money.'

'Don't, Max! Please don't do it. I don't want you to.'

'Hey, it's no sweat.' He grinned, full of casual ease about going up all that distance in a plane and freefalling through the sky. Jumping against her wishes, full of carefree confidence that he was indestructible. An action hero, a guy who could pretend he wasn't mortal at all. Just like her ex. 'I won't be long.'

'I really can't watch,' she said honestly. 'I can't stand it, it makes me feel sick. I don't like it, Max.'

'Then get off home and I'll call you later. But don't worry. I'm an old hand. I don't even have bumpy landings.'

Max ran off towards the plane.

She turned away, unable to watch him go. He was experienced; it was in his blood. Would this relationship blow up in her face as it had done with Grant?

★ ★ ★

After brief farewells, with Anya declining a trip to the pub to celebrate their endeavours, she headed home with her mum and Callum in tow.

Anya made a detour to stop at a

chemist in Loch Dinny, under the fabricated excuse of picking up some cough syrup and flu remedy as she felt something coming on. In truth she was picking up a pregnancy test. She stopped in Loch Dinny because she didn't want to be recognised, and at all her local chemists she was too well known to evade detection.

The whole time, it felt like she had fallen down a hole into someone else's life. It couldn't be happening to her.

She'd given up the dream of being able to have a child of her own.

She didn't date. Let alone sleep with men.

So why was this happening?

The thought haunted her all the way home. This length of delay in her cycle had never happened, ever.

She hid the pregnancy test right at the bottom of her bag. She hoped what used to happen would repeat itself. In the days when she and Grant were trying for a baby, whenever Anya bought a test, her period invariably started a few hours later. Today she willed her period to appear, and put its absence down to stress and coincidence.

She hadn't been sick again, but did have persistent tiredness. She was still queasy every now and then. She silenced the annoying backing track in her head.

She dropped her mum off and then returned to the cottage, her mind still full of pregnancy thoughts. After making Callum's tea, playing with him and reading to him, she ran a bath. With Cal in bed asleep, she opened up the pregnancy test packet.

The last time she'd stared at a pregnancy predictor test like this she'd been with Grant, wishing and hoping for a positive. But the result had been a negative, and she'd cried and cried. Anya followed the directions as guided by the illustrations anyway, and left it on the side.

The phone rang and she went to answer it. When she reached it, the line stayed live but ominously silent, and panic struck her.

'Hello?'

Silence met her ears.

'Max? Katie? Mum? Who's there?'

The line clicked dead and the caller hung up, reflecting the at-work pattern. Her sense of panic and loathing went into freefall. She felt sick and weak and utterly flooded by dread.

She'd had no calls since she'd been off work, and she'd been feeling elated. This call was at home, at her cottage, flagging up that her problem hadn't disappeared: it had worsened.

Anya took a sharp breath, her vision wobbling. It must be Joe, and if he knew where Callum was, what was stopping him dropping by any time he liked?

What did he want from them? At heart, she knew it was to see her son, to cause disturbance in their lives. Maybe money, too. A sob burst from her chest and she hurried to the bathroom to check the taps were off. She was about to drain her bath when she saw the test lying on the side, and stopped in her tracks.

The tiny green dot indicated a positive pregnancy test. The dot she'd wished for so hard before was in stark definition to the white plastic.

While joy buoyed and perplexed her . . . could her life get any messier and hard to deal with?

'It just can't be.' Anya rummaged in the packaging to recheck the instructions and results information. 'I'm pregnant!'

Her heart jumped with elation — there was already a tiny life inside her that held infinite promise. The thing she'd prayed for, cried about, and wished and wished and wished for with all her heart.

Tears ran freely down her face as she stared at the indicator. She may not have jumped out of a plane like she'd planned. But she was going to have Max Calder's baby, and for that she could only be happy, amazed and grateful. The miracle baby she'd thought could never happen to her just had.

'What have you done?' she whispered.

The telephone rang again.

Startled, Anya pulled herself back to the here and now, and went to answer it in the kitchen, still in a state of fight or flight.

The line stayed silent.

'Who is this?' she demanded angrily. 'Stop harassing me!'

'What's wrong? Who's harassing you?' Max's stern voice demanded in shock.

Anya sucked in air. 'Sorry, Max, I didn't realise it was you.'

'Who has been pestering you and why haven't you told me anything about this?' His voice hardened. 'I knew there was something wrong. You'd better tell me what's going on, because I'm coming over there right now, Anya, and I intend to get to the bottom of this.'

Anya stared hard at the back of her hands as she made tea for them both. Thick, strong tea. The kind she knew that if she even sipped would cause sickness to sweep her into the bathroom in seconds.

You should tell him. Tell him what you know. That you're pregnant!

'I've had a few crank calls,' she managed instead. 'Someone hanging up without speaking. It's nothing to worry about. Seriously.'

And I'm having your baby.

The words kept repeating themselves in her head, but she wasn't ready to say them out loud to him. Yet still they persisted.

Max looked utterly frustrated and angrier than she'd imagined he would be. 'As senior partner, I make it my business to know these things. All our staff concern me; their private issues can impact on their professional life. Did you ever plan on telling me?'

'There's nothing to tell.'

'Is this why you backed out of the jump?' he demanded. 'Have you been worrying about these calls and keeping it secret?'

Anya shook her head. She wasn't about to admit her suspicions to Max that the perpetrator was Callum's father Joe, either. He'd most likely insist on getting the authorities involved, and she wasn't ready for that. She needed to be sure first.

'Then it won't matter if I hear all the evidence and help you put measures in place to deal with it.'

Max's tone told of uncompromising stubbornness. There was no way she could flannel him, not from the mood he was displaying tonight. Why, she wondered, was he so very angry over this?

'Look, I've had a few calls, but nothing's been said. The caller hangs up.'

'How many calls?'

She swiftly debated whether or not to lie. 'Seven.'

'Seven calls! That's harassment.'

'Silence isn't harassment. It's an irritating prankster.'

'And how do you deal with these calls? Do you talk or hang up or what?'

'I can hardly slam the phone down at work.'

Anya winced at her own unintended slip. She hadn't meant to let Max know that she'd received the calls at work. She should have covered it up. Made him think it was only at the cottage. Now he knew it was at the surgery too, he'd be going to extremes because he had the authority to do so. Damn her thoughtless tongue.

Max looked murderous. 'You mean to tell me you've been receiving crank calls at the surgery and you've never reported it? I'm appalled at you. What about protecting yourself, your son?' He was beside her in seconds.

'Don't lecture me. I was handling it in my own way.'

'You think? Last time I was here, you were in a terrible state about the possibility that your son's violent biological father might track you down. These developments didn't strike you as significant?'

He'd have made a brilliant barrister. She could imagine him in court, wearing a gorgeous sharp suit and stern facade. Immoveable and principled on issues such as this.

'I'm not happy with this. I don't think it's safe you being here alone. I'm going to insist you come to my place.'

'Callum's in bed, Max. I'm not waking him.'

'Then I'll stay here with you.'

Anya groaned. 'You don't have to do that.'

His eyes were dark probes that bored into her, leaving her in no doubt he wouldn't back down. 'I think I do. And first thing Monday, I'm putting procedures in place against crank calls at work. You should have alerted me right from the beginning.'

'It might just be kids playing silly games.'

'It might not. And we need to legislate for that risk. Your photo was published in a national paper. You're an attractive woman, which makes you a target.'

Before the night was out he'd discussed the matter with the local police — with a passing mention of Callum's adoptive status — spoken to her telephone services provider to put steps in place to bar the caller, and insisted he slept on the couch.

She eyed him over the top of the pile of pillows and blankets she presented him with from the hallway cupboard. She still felt pulses of attraction when it came to Max. Even now, she was wishing things were different, but she'd forced herself into her own tight corner. She'd told him she was principled and could see no future for them as a couple.

'You're sure you'll be comfortable?' she asked, noting the way her breathing hitched at his proximity.

'Don't worry about me. I'm happy

we've alerted people who can stop this.' He looked at her hard. 'Now, tell me truthfully, why didn't you go through with the jump today? Why cry off after all that preparation?'

Anya paused, torn. Now was the time to just say it. To admit the truth, her reasons. To come clean about her confirmed condition now.

But she couldn't. Not yet. He was going to Italy, and he should make up his own mind about the job. She didn't want him to buckle under the pressure of a baby, to give up his dreams for her. Maybe he'd decide to stay? If he took the job, she'd tell him and insist he follow his heart. She'd tell him soon, most definitely.

'I realised I have limitations.'

'But why are you so intent on limiting yourself? I had faith you could do it. Like I have faith in us. But you constantly back off. I don't understand why you've so little faith in yourself.'

'Because I've learned that sometimes it's better not to hope for too much.'

She sighed. 'I never told you this before, but I saw Grant's new girlfriend at his funeral. She was carrying his baby when he died, newly pregnant. It was terrible and tragic. Part of me just felt bitter. I only realised then he'd always have placed his family second. The risks came first.'

'I'm sorry, Anya. But you have to get over what happened between you and Grant. You have to see we have a future beyond that.'

You take risks, and it squeezes my heart every time.

'If you need anything, help yourself,' she told him, and surprised herself by putting a hand protectively over her tummy. 'I'm upstairs if you need me.'

'Goodnight.'

Max removed his sweater, revealing a T-shirt that defined those muscles in the lamplight. Then he turned away before punching his pillow into a suitable shape for his head. She turned her own back rather than embarrass herself.

'Goodnight,' she repeated softly. 'And thanks for helping me.'

The father of the child inside her disapproved of her. And there was nothing she could do about that unless she went back on her principles. She'd forced him there of her own accord.

16

The next morning it was raining cats, dogs and opened floodgates. Callum had a date at eleven for a birthday party at a friend's home, and all morning he'd been in a state of hyped-up anticipation, jumping on the spot like a toy with a spring.

If she'd heard the phrase 'Can we go now, Mummy?' once, Anya had heard it several hundred times.

Add to that morning sickness that even the smell of toast seemed to aggravate, and she wasn't in the best frame of mind. Plus there was the hollow recognition that today was the first day of her life that she'd ever woken up in bed highly aware of her special status. She was pregnant.

Max had left after breakfast, making his disapproval of her handling of the mystery phone calls very clear. They'd barely exchanged half a dozen civil sentences. Before he left, though, he promised to make further calls to the local police station on the topic of her harassment.

Now all she could do was wait and see if the phone calls stopped.

And, of course, take Callum to his party. If she didn't stop listening to his excitement soon, she'd be driven to down headache pills, or take him to the party two hours before it was even due to start.

★ ★ ★

Callum left the party at four that afternoon. His friend Gregor MacKenzie's home was a sea of balloons, streamers, bunting and small excited running children.

Gregor's mum looked tired but good-humoured. 'Next year I'm hiring a hall. Parties in the house are too scary.'

Anya checked her pockets for her

keys, then realised she must have left them in the ignition, which wasn't like her. But then she'd been in a rush, and her mind seemed to be only half on what she was doing lately.

Anyway, the MacKenzies lived out in the wilds in an old farmhouse up a long gravel drive. There'd be scant danger of car theft here.

Callum ran out into his mother's waiting arms, laden with party bags filled with cake and goodies. 'That was a brilliant party, Mummy,' he enthused. 'Can we come back soon?'

'I'm glad you had such a wonderful time. Say thanks to Gregor's mum!'

Callum obliged, shooting off down the drive at a rate of knots.

She was relieved to note her hunch about the keys had been right when she saw them dangling from the ignition. Only after she had strapped Callum into his child seat did she notice that her bag was missing from the front passenger seat. She racked her brains on her earlier movements. Surely she'd remember where she'd put it? If she had lost her handbag it would be a nightmare; replacing keys and bank cards was a hassle she could well do without.

'Concentrate,' she told herself sternly. 'You're starting to lose your marbles.'

'Marbles,' said Callum, quick as a fox round the side of a henhouse. 'Can we play with my marbles when we get back home? Please?'

'OK,' she agreed, praying she wasn't going to hear a chorus of pleading for marbles all the way back to Alderwick. 'We'll get your marble maze out and have fun when we get back, and hopefully you'll work off the cake energy burst.'

Anya smiled into the rear-view mirror at her son as a vague trickle of unease whirred inside as she racked her brains. Was she doing things without remembering, as well as forgetting important things like keys and bags?

When she drew up outside the cottage, helped Callum from the car and went inside via the spare back-door key on her car-key fob, she realised she'd forgotten to rummage for her mislaid handbag now too.

It was only as she did so that she distinctly remembered leaving by the front door, and using her key to do so. She did have her bag with her. So where was it?

The whirring unease started to build as she struggled to subdue her son's marble hunt. Her bag was gone. Someone must have taken it. Had she been followed?

Fear spiked hard inside. Now that her anonymity had been compromised, the inevitable panic snuck up on her, forcing terror into her system.

And then she saw it. Lying on the kitchen counter by the door. And a wrapped bouquet of bright flowers lay close by. Her bag. Not gone, not stuck in the car by mistake, but at home. How?

She was thinking these words just as the door shut behind her, and she jumped near out of her skin.

'Anya?' an unfamiliar male voice said behind her. 'It's only me. I bought you flowers.'

Her heart was hammering in her chest as she turned.

'William,' he continued. 'You remember me?'

'Sorry?'

The last she'd heard about William Mays was that he'd got a job in Dubai and was working for an oil company out there. Seeing him the other week had been unexpected, as she hadn't known he was back. She also remembered Max meeting him at The Crofters.

Something wasn't right here. They barely knew each other. Why on earth would William let himself uninvited into her home? Snoop around, leave flowers?

'What are you doing in my house?' she demanded. 'Did you leave me those flowers?'

'I wanted to talk to you at the MacKenzies'. I was waiting in the car.

But I didn't want to scare you. You mean too much to me.'

'This isn't scary?' Her voice was a squeak. 'What do you want, William? You've nearly given me a heart attack. I should call the police. You can't let yourself into people's homes uninvited.'

'I only want to talk. It's been a long time.'

Not long enough.

'Did you like the flowers?' he continued, coming closer.

'You shouldn't be buying me flowers, William. What are you doing here?'

Her thoughts were running ahead to Callum. Why was William here in her house? What did he intend?

'You're always so busy. Rushing to pick up your son or to get to work. I never have enough time to speak to you properly,' he complained, watching her. 'But you know I've always liked you.'

She'd known William by sight a long time. He'd lived in the village for a decade, but he was an incomer. He'd been married and then divorced his wife years before. One night Isla Stuart had held a dinner party at which Anya had been placed beside William, and they'd got chatting.

He'd seemed friendly enough that night, though there had never been any spark there for her. She'd gently declined his offers of a date, and seen him a few times afterwards. Now she recalled, he had asked her out at each opportunity.

But there had never been anything between them. He'd been gone fourteen months, and she'd heard it said that he'd hit the big time with his fantastic job in Dubai. She'd privately wished him well with his fresh start. He'd had a lot of bitterness about his acrimonious split with his wife, and her new relationship and pregnancy with another man had hit him hard.

'I've liked you a long time,' he said, half-accusingly. 'But you're like Franny. You give me smiles and then leave me to bleed!'

'I'm not like your wife, William. I'm

just a local nurse. There's nothing between us.'

William edged closer. 'But there could be. If you'd let me take you out. Or is this just because Max Calder got in there first?'

Ripples of fear ran down Anya's spine. Sheer terror consumed her as she rallied for the power to make suitable conversation, aware that her son Callum was upstairs rummaging for the promised marble maze and could at any minute walk back in on this sinister exchange.

'I think you should leave,' she said, trying not to make too much eye contact. He really did look anxious. And his anxiety was making her nervous; William Mays clearly had a lot of problems he needed resolving. She didn't feel inclined to make a cup of tea or start any psychobabble now. Not when Cal was potentially at risk.

William fixed her with a dark brooding gaze. 'Don't you remember, I got us tickets to the ballet *Coppélia*?

Because you said you liked it. But you still turned me down. What would it take for you to say yes?'

To think she'd thought he was a nice guy.

'I had an adoption agency meeting commitment on that date. You didn't check first. William, have you been calling me on the phone recently and staying silent?'

He nodded. 'I just wanted to ask you out, Anya. To take you to dinner. I've been working up the nerve. Wondering what's going on between you and Max Calder.'

He loped towards her so swiftly she gasped and jumped back.

'I won't hurt you,' he said, reaching out to stroke her hand.

She pulled backwards on reflex. She couldn't bear him so near. She wanted him gone from her home. On impulse, her hand went to her tummy, to conceal and protect it.

'William, please go!'

To think she'd imagined this man

was good company. Was her judgement that awry?

Suddenly he leant forwards and touched her face. Anya leapt back. She couldn't bear for this man to touch her. This man, with his insinuations of wanting her in an entirely inappropriate way, and claiming that she'd led him on in some imagined manner.

'I barely know you; why would you come to my home and scare me?

'You're just like Franny. You twist the things I say.'

Then, to her surprise, he stepped unsteadily back and doubled up in pain.

'William?'

His face contorted as he clutched his chest.

'Not feeling good . . . ' he stammered. 'I've been getting these pains . . . ' He doubled up again as another spasm consumed him.

His teeth chattered and his eyes started to roll in his head.

'William!'

Her tormentor slumped onto his knees on the floor and passed out.

She stared at him for a moment, uncomprehending. Her first instinct was to run, but then the nurse in her took over. At speed, and with little thought for her safety, she reached out to grab her mobile phone from her pocket. Shaky fingers pressed Max's name and the call button as she rushed upstairs to find her son.

To think she'd assumed all this could be connected to Callum's past. Yet all the time it had been about her. In trying to protect her boy, she'd left both of them open to risk.

She connected with Max in half a dozen rings.

'Max, can you get straight over here? There's an intruder in my house. I need help. He's having some kind of fit.'

'I'm on my way, hold tight. Lock yourselves in a room if needs be,' he replied quickly.

She stuffed the phone in her pocket as she pulled Callum close, complete with marble maze box, and dashed back downstairs.

'Stay in the dining room and wait for Mummy,' she instructed him.

His lip wavered, clearly upset because she was. Anya held it together and kissed his head before telling him again in earnest, 'Max is coming. As soon as that doorbell rings, you let him in. There's a sick man in the kitchen, and I need to look after him. Do you understand?'

Callum nodded sombrely and she ran back into the kitchen to find William lying prostrate on the floor. His seizure caused convulsions. But it was a seizure that was saving her from heaven knew what!

'William, can you hear me?' she asked him going to his side.

He shuddered violently. And, to her surprise, she managed to summon professional calm. 'Help is on the way.'

His condition looked serious now, his face ashen, body shaking. She tried to make him comfortable though she

269

couldn't be sure what was wrong. To her intense relief, it wasn't long before she heard the doorbell and then Callum's high voice in the hall.

'Let me deal with this,' said Max from the doorway. 'Go! Your son needs you. And I want you out of danger.'

17

Max had observed Anya's hands. They were shaking like tree branches in a storm. But he couldn't spare the time to comfort her and Callum. He had a job to do.

He was a doctor, and while a part of him despised this intruder, he also realised he had a duty of care towards him, just the same as with any patient. But what had he intended? To hold Anya and Callum captive? *Worse?*

Max pulled himself back into doctor mode. It was William; he recognised him now. Crouching beside the patient, he looked at the evidence before him, checking for a pulse and noting his skin colour. At least he hadn't been lying here for long.

At first Max had assumed he was unconscious, but now he could plainly see the patient was having some sort of seizure. Gently, Max loosened William's shirt collar, and turned him on his side to keep his airway free of saliva.

'Is it epilepsy?' Anya asked from the hallway.

'I'm not sure,' he replied. 'Of course, we've no way of knowing if there's a history of epilepsy.'

'There can't be.' She shook her head. 'He used to do taxi work at one time. Plus, I've treated him a few times, I'd have noted if he had a history of it. Shall I call an ambulance?'

'And the police,' Max agreed. 'This is an intruder, after all. Not a house guest.'

Anya flipped open her phone to make the call.

Max sifted through the evidence before him. If William had epilepsy, it would be unlikely he could drive for a living because of the risk of seizure behind the wheel. Many things could trigger an attack. But Max wanted to be careful. What if it wasn't epilepsy at all?

Anya reappeared. 'They're on their way.'

'How did he get in?' Max asked, turning to meet her gaze.

'I'm not sure. He must have followed me to the party and stolen my bag from my car. When I got back with Callum, he was already here.' She tried to keep her voice level. 'It was so frightening. I'm not sure what he intended to do. I'm still reeling.'

'You were lucky. And so, it seems, is he. You saved him from an unknown fate.'

William seemed to be waking up.

Max bent over him reassuringly. 'Don't worry, William, an ambulance is on its way.'

The patient seemed confused and disoriented, so Max advised him to stay still and not try to talk. He removed his sweatshirt and put it around William's shoulders for extra warmth.

Soon Anya and Max saw the welcome blue flashing lights of an ambulance through the cottage window.

He briefly discussed what had occurred with the paramedic team who quickly set to work and helped the patient into the ambulance.

'These are trained paramedics. They'll take you into Tynedrammy Infirmary. The doctors there will run a few tests and scans. I'm afraid I'm also alerting the police about what happened here today.'

But William still seemed too dazed to take much of the conversation in.

Max gave her a warning look that told he thought she'd had a lucky reprieve. As soon as they were alone, he pulled her into strong arms. He held her tightly against his chest and tried to resist the urge to kiss her.

She'd scared him to death. Did she make herself so foolishly vulnerable on purpose? Lately she was turning his entire world upside down and twisting his emotions into unsalvageable knots.

Anya pulled away before their lips could meet.

Max let out a groan of frustration.

'Do you know what you put me through?'

'Don't make this any harder.' He could sense she was close to tears and a bundle of shaky nerves.

He whirled on her with angry eyes that bored into her soft blue-grey ones. There was nothing soft about how this woman was treating him: fending him off, knocking his advances back.

'You've made your position clear enough, haven't you? You're too busy fighting ghosts from the past. That's where we're different — I've moved on. You need to do that too. And until that happens, there's no hope for us — you're right. We have no future while you remain this closed off.' He glared at her. 'Don't worry, I'll keep my distance.'

To his chagrin, she burst into tears in front of him.

Reluctantly, Max went to her door to let the police in. 'But I'll stay with you until all this is over,' he added. 'Now do you see why it's important not to think you know all the answers? If the police had known about the calls earlier, it's possible none of this would have happened.'

Max spent the next ten minutes helping Anya deal with questions from the police. He saw the remorse and fear in her expression. He even noted the excited but frightened look on Callum's face as he peered around the corner of the dining room door, and that bothered him too.

When the police had gone, he took Anya back to the lounge and forced her to stand and listen to him.

'I need to say some things. When will you listen? You're so busy playing Miss Independent that you sometimes get it wrong. I can't operate in your pragmatic, detached way. You can't always decide how to react. Sometimes emotions come along and change things, and sometimes you have to do things you don't want to for the greater good — like admitting when there's a problem with prank calls. Where's the sense in denial?'

He watched her bite her lip, staving off the tears again.

Max could sense she was getting upset. He was aware that her son was sitting in the next room during this exchange.

'Wait a minute,' he said, walking to the dining room only to find Cal playing with his marble maze, intent on the small glass balls.

'Can you play with me now, Max?' Callum asked him with watchful eyes.

'We'll be with you in a minute, son. You've been a really good boy today,' Max said to Anya's beloved child. A boy who was meaning more and more to him with every passing day. A boy he'd go to great lengths to protect. Max walked back into the lounge and found her staring shocked and upset into space with tears in her eyes.

'Callum's fine,' he told her. 'I don't mean to blame you. I'm trying to tell you that sometimes you don't handle things as well as you think.'

Her tear-clouded blue grey gaze lifted to his. 'I've coped alone for so long, I can't avoid doing it now,' she whispered. 'It's instinctive. It's how I survived and got through my life crises. I switch into automatic coping mode. But I don't expect you to understand that.'

'Maybe I can if you let me,' he said baldly. 'Do you trust me?'

'Of course.'

'Then what's the problem here? Why are you pushing me away, sending me to Italy — as if you can't get me far enough away?'

'Have you ever felt so powerless that you don't even trust yourself? I coped by denying myself. I've trained myself, schooled my brain to do it. Can't you see that I only push you away because realising what I can't have hurts too much?'

'Do you really think I can't understand? After what I've been through?' he replied sharply. 'With my background, I know the anger caused by losing control. But it doesn't mean you can't hope. It doesn't necessitate closing all systems down to a brighter future.'

'But I'm scared. You take risks. You climb mountains, you bungee-jump for fun. I can't handle the thought of waiting at home for the phone to ring with bad news.' Anya shook her head. 'My heart can't take the dents. It's too fragile. And Callum has to be my first priority, I can't let him down.'

Max sighed. 'I'm not asking you to let me usurp Callum in your heart. I'm asking to let me care for both of you. Maybe I do take risks, but it doesn't mean I can't be careful. Besides, now that I've found you and Cal, I don't want to be careless anymore. You both mean too much to me.'

Max shoved his hand through his hair and stared out of the window. The hard lines of his body showed his pent-up strain.

'I've decided to accept that job in Italy,' he told her bluntly. He saw the tears in her eyes when she looked at him and it broke his heart. 'I can't keep coming back only to be pushed away. It's hurting us both.'

Her smile wobbled enough for him to know it was her self-reliance act. The one she wouldn't let slip. The one she felt her life depended on. 'You've a big future ahead of you,' she said quietly. 'You should go for it, truly. Congratulations, Max.'

'Don't!' said Max raggedly. 'We both know it's not what I want.'

'I'm sorry I've been so stupid, Max. I always think I can handle things my way, but it seems I can't. And I've got . . . I've got something else I have to tell you.'

He looked at her quizzically.

'After the parachute jump, I did a pregnancy test. My period had been late.' She paused. 'Max, I'm pregnant. And it's your baby.'

Max held her apart from him. He couldn't believe his ears. He'd just told her he was going to Italy, that he'd finally taken the decision — and now she delivered a bombshell like this?

Max pulled away as if she was made of burning coals.

'You're pregnant? How can you just tell me this? Why on earth haven't you told me before? You've broken my heart, torn me in pieces worrying about you, and now this . . . '

He could not disguise the bitterness in his voice. He felt the pain of her betrayal in every sinew and pore. Max watched as she began to cry, and felt an inevitable guilt at having upset her again.

'I'm frightened of so many things,' she whispered. 'I don't even know where to start. I didn't want you declining the Italian medical job because of me, just because I was carrying your child.'

'Wasn't that for me to decide?' he fumed.

'I wasn't thinking clearly. Since I took the test, I've hardly been able to think in straight lines.'

'Well, you've told me now. You shouldn't feel powerless. From my perspective, you've been holding all the cards on our relationship for some time. Taking charge and keeping me outside the boundary wall. You just have to face up to your fears and accept you're only human, and that sometimes life can turn out OK. It's worth trying because it can go right. And now that I know you're having my baby, I can do something about it — I don't intend to sit back and let you walk out of my life. Even if you don't want me, your baby will need its father.'

Anya shattered in his arms and gave way to tears. Max let her cry. Crying was the best medicine in this case. She needed it, she just needed time to realise how much she was kidding herself, how she'd miss out on something so good it left him breathless, hurt and frustrated. All because she refused to see he was right.

'I'm sorry, Max. I'm so sorry.'

'That makes two of us,' said Max, and sighed. 'Now we have to decide what we're going to do.'

18

Three days later, Anya was expecting Katie to drop by and visit her.

At the sound of a knock on her cottage door, she jumped and closed the pregnancy magazine she'd been reading, guiltily stashing it away at the back of a kitchen drawer.

Katie had told her she'd be round at eight, but it seemed she was early. Her friend had also claimed she had some surprise news, though Anya had something of a sense of trepidation about that. She'd had enough shocks in the last few weeks to last her a decade at least.

'Hi, come in,' she told her friend as Katie presented her with a tissue-wrapped bottle of wine. She accepted it with a smile, but realised she'd have to find a suitable excuse not to partake of any alcohol.

'You're still looking pale,' her friend told her sympathetically. 'Feeling any better?'

'A bit. It still hasn't sunk in properly, to be honest.'

Katie followed her through to the lounge, removed her jacket and sank gratefully back onto the sofa.

'It must have been quite an ordeal for you,' said Katie, eyeing her thoughtfully. 'The whole village is reeling. So shocking.'

'I'd hoped the whole village didn't already know,' Anya replied.

'A figure of speech . . . ' Katie waved a hand and then fished inside her expansive straw bag to remove an enormous box of chocolate pralines and a case that looked like it contained a DVD.

'Gifts,' she announced. 'Something I wanted you to see. Stick this in the DVD player. The other ones are for snacking as we chat.'

Coming back from the kitchen with a wineglass for Katie and a bottle of sparkling water for herself, she took the DVD and obliged.

'It's the parachute jump video,' Katie explained. 'It's fantastic, thought you'd like to see it. Only pause it for now because I need to talk first.'

Katie looked quizzically at the bottle of wine. When Anya said she wasn't drinking, Katie admitted that she wasn't either.

'The thing is, I've something to tell you,' Katie said. 'These last few months I've been keeping something to myself. I want to talk about it now.'

'What is it?'

'Last winter I noticed a lump on my breast in the shower. It was small but painful. At the time I thought it was nothing, but raised it with my GP at Glenfields anyway.'

Anya nodded. Katie's GP there had been Max.

'Max referred me to Tynedrammy for tests, ultrasound and a mammogram. I then had a biopsy to remove the lump. I thought it might go further and that I'd have to have a mastectomy. The great news is that I came through clear. I'm still getting regular checks, but . . . ' Katie crossed her fingers. 'So far, so good. But it's made me appreciate living for the present.'

'Oh Katie,' Anya gasped. 'And you dealt with all that on your own?'

'I didn't want everyone pussyfooting around me and pitying me. So I dealt with it myself. One step at a time. And the good news is, it's looking positive.'

Anya leaned over to pull her friend close for a hug. 'Katie!'

Tears welled up without her being able to stop them. She'd been so wrapped up in her own life — her son, getting on with being a single mum, Max — she'd failed to notice her best friend might be going through far worse . . .

'Hey, stop the waterworks! It's not why I'm telling you this. I want you to be happy. I can and will get through this. And it's the reason I did the charity jump. It gave me something to work for and helped take my mind off the cancer scare, and for that I'm grateful. And I'm sorry I railroaded you into taking part, because that was unfair of me!'

'I'm only sorry I backed out.'

Katie pulled a dismissive face. 'It doesn't matter. All the pledged sponsorship money has come in anyway. Adoption Support has had a massive profile push as a result, and best of all, it's given me a taste for adventure. Going through health investigations has made me see we have to grasp our chances!'

Anya's shaky hand on her water glass gave her away and in spite of all her inclinations not to let herself crumble, the next second she found she was weeping, sobbing into her hands.

'Anya! What's up?'

Her emotions had been haywire for days. Partly due to the shock incident with William Mays, but also partly, Anya suspected, from the way her early pregnancy hormones were dancing a scary, erratic tune. These days she was weepy one minute, elated the next.

'Oh, Katie. I can't even begin to tell you!'

Katie edged closer and took her hand. 'Try me. It's what friends are for. I can always offer you an ear, a hug, an encouraging word.'

Anya sighed deeply, but knew she had to tell *someone*.

'I'm pregnant.' She met her friend's gaze. 'I know it sounds mad but it's true.'

Katie said nothing but gaped. Finally, she whispered, 'After all you went through?'

'I can still hardly believe it myself. One minute I'm ecstatic, the next I'm terrified.'

Katie shrugged her shoulders in a gesture that asked a million questions but didn't vocalise a single one. 'Miracles can always happen.'

'Max is the father.' Anya felt the tears run afresh. 'And yes, I've told him. He'd just accepted a job in Turin, and now he's asked me for time because he needs space to think. He feels betrayed by me. I didn't tell him at first because I didn't want to wreck his life out of honour and duty. Now I feel like I gate-crashed his life with a one-night stand.'

'And that's all that's between you? One night?' Katie probed.

'One night of passion — and after all these years hoping and wishing for a baby, I finally get my dream coming true, but in entirely the wrong circumstances. Ironic, isn't it?'

'But whatever the circumstances, you and I both know Max isn't the wrong guy. He's the right one for you.'

'Yes,' Anya croaked softly. 'He is. I love him so much and yet I'm terrified I could lose him over this. Terrified that he'll destroy me. He's like Grant in a way. And yet I never loved Grant this way.'

Katie shook her head. 'Speaking from my experiences with him as my GP, Max is an amazing man. Compassionate, dependable, everything any woman could ever wish for . . . and sexy too! Here, look at this.'

Katie rose and picked up the remote to press play on her parachute spectacular.

The pair sat in silence as they watched. The piece had been professionally edited and was well put together. Katie appeared in an introductory piece about the charity and the reasoning behind their efforts — she also revealed her 'secret' about her cancer challenge as being her motivation to take this scary step.

When Max appeared before the camera, Anya's heart leapt in her chest. The serious air he had when he talked on camera about his love of parachuting and his regard for the charity were inspiring and made her pride swell. He even made a small speech about his own background.

'I was lucky to come through the adoption process. Through it, I learned love and hope and courage. Any charity that supports this kind of human *endeavour has my utmost respect.'*

Anya watched the film, forcing back tears as she saw her own fearful expression, faced with the jump. She watched her eyes continually flick to Max; there was raw need and love in that gaze. She'd never before realised how strong her feelings were for him — was she so very transparent at heart?

Thinking back to what she'd had to go through, yes, she probably was entitled to be needy. She just hadn't realised that she didn't hide it so well around Max.

And then she remembered the thoughts that had been running through her brain that day of the jump. The realisation that she might in fact be carrying a child had only dawned on her properly that morning. No wonder her face was a conundrum of anxiety.

Katie switched off the TV. 'You love him,' she said simply, as though she had read Anya's thoughts. 'More than I've ever seen you love anyone besides your son! Why would you doubt that?'

'I do love him, don't I?' Anya nodded, holding back the tears. She scanned the room in frustration. 'What am I doing? What am I going to do, Katie?'

'Tell him the truth. Tell him the daredevil stuff scares you, but you still love him and you're going to put your faith in everything that he is. Then let yourself fall into his arms because he loves you right back!' Katie smiled sunnily. 'Trust me on this, it'll work out.'

'But I worry every single time Callum sets foot outside the door. Loving a man who takes risks like Max fills me with fear.'

'Loving anyone with your whole heart is like that,' said Katie firmly. As someone who'd lost her husband seven years before, she knew that more than most people. Katie's husband Alec had died tragically during a shock car crash that had shaken the community. That was what always inspired Anya about Katie: her friend's resilience in the face of everything she'd had to contend with.

Anya sighed and wiped her tear tracks dry. 'But could Max love me? Has he got space for me and Callum? And a new child already underway?'

Katie's piercing eyes bored into hers. 'Ask him and you'll soon have your answer.'

'But I don't want to trap him. I didn't want to start an affair because I was reluctant to upend Callum's life, though now ironically that's going to happen anyway, whether I like it or not.' She sighed. 'I do want this baby, Katie, make no mistake. It's like a miracle. But I can't spoil things for Max: he's had such a hard past, he deserves a sky-high future. Besides, I can't bear his charity. I suffered people's pity at not conceiving until it made me sick to the stomach. I guess I have issues with charity and people giving out platitudes when they don't have the faintest clue.'

'And you really think you can let Max go off to work in Italy while you have his child here?' Katie demanded. 'Remember, he and I have a special bond; he's shared things with me on a personal level. He's a man who values family above all else. Go and tell him how much you love him, and the rest will sort itself out.'

Anya ran a hand through her hair. 'Goodness, Katie, I haven't thought further ahead than the next few hours. What a mess I've made of everything.'

'Then it's time to plan the next few hours with precision. I'll babysit for your sleeping boy. I can stay the night here. Go and tell the man you love him. Take a chance on love. You've found a wonderful man, and just because life's been unkind so far, you should always hope things may change.'

Anya tried her best not to cry again but the tears rolled afresh as she hugged her friend close, knowing there was a tiny life inside her tummy that would be affected by the outcome of the next few hours more than it could ever know.

'It's time for my leap of faith, isn't it? Only this one's more painful than jumping from a plane. I know he's worth it. He's worth every gut-wrenching moment. Because I love him! Knowing that has terrified me into denying it from the start. And now I have to take my leap into the unknown.'

★ ★ ★

There's something you need to know. I want this baby, I don't want you to go to Turin, I want you here, and I want you in my life. As my husband. Till death us do part.

She said the words in her head all the way over to Cara Cottage, her emotions churning wildly.

He came to the door wearing nothing but a white towel wrapped about his waist, his hair wet, fresh from the shower. He was holding a T-shirt as though she had interrupted him dressing.

'Anya!' he exclaimed, clearly surprised. He pulled the T-shirt over his head. 'Come in. Sorry, I'm in the middle of getting scrubbed up. I've been working on the bike. How are you feeling?'

She smiled weakly. 'Don't ask, just let me come in and say what I have to.'

Max's puzzlement was clear but he entreated her inside with a sweep of his arm.

Anya stood in his tiled hallway, realising she loved this man, was carrying his child, and yet had never even seen the inside of his home.

Cara Cottage: a place that was home to a man so dear to her it squeezed her heart. A man who was even now mentally preparing to leave her and go away to Italy.

'I need to say I'm sorry,' she began. 'That I'm a fool — '

' 'Fool' is harsh.'

She held up a hand. 'Don't even dare stop me!'

'But I'm a daredevil, you're forgetting.' He smiled. 'I'm intrepid, I take risks.'

He didn't seem to be taking this as seriously as she'd hoped.

'Max!' she exclaimed, exasperated. 'I'm trying to say I'm sorry. I've been so wrapped up in my own cloistered cocoon of me and Callum I wouldn't listen to you or let you in. Because Grant made me scared to open myself up to danger, I was petrified to even try loving someone else.'

'Progress,' Max remarked coolly, as he towel-dried his short dark hair.

'I'm ripping my soul out here, and you're acting like you're on something.'

'Maybe I am, my love,' he replied. 'You're here, and that's headier than any drug known to mankind or the medical profession.'

Anya shook her head in bewilderment and summoned fresh courage to restart her soliloquy afresh.

'So I'm here to tell you I love you. I care. That you matter, and I want you in my life.' Her voice began to crack and his face melted as he reached out to her. 'I'm so happy about this baby of ours, I could burst with joy.'

She bit her lip, then went for the jugular. She'd been through so damn much in recent weeks that finally getting it all out there felt good, like blood-letting. She needed to be free of this draining truth inside.

'I want to be in your life, Max. Me and Callum and our baby,' she said firmly. 'Could you give up your dream job for us?'

Max paused for a full twenty seconds. Twenty seconds where he just watched her and she couldn't read him.

Then he said, 'It could never have been any different. Not for me, you're all I want. I've been waiting for you to admit that our relationship could work. That you could trust me to be a father to our children. And to come round here and let me take you in my arms.'

* * *

All he'd ever wanted was for this amazing woman to wake up, and show him the vulnerability she hid away inside like a guilty secret. Admit to their mutual attraction and need. And here she was.

She had so much power, if only she would realise it. Power over him. To cheer his soul with a smile, or fell him with a kiss.

'We're having this baby and giving Cal the dad he deserves,' Max stated plainly, hugging her to him. 'You and me. No doubts, no questions.' The woman he loved. 'And no Turin.

'You've had me in knots,' he continued, kissing her hair. 'Tight knots of frustrated agony. Didn't you notice how emotional I was when you said you didn't want to do the parachute jump?'

Anya shook her head, nonplussed.

'And couldn't you see how angry I was that night, when I found out about the phone calls? I'd been on the point of coming round and confronting you about everything. I nearly came over to see you three times.' He regarded her with solemn honesty.

'Why?'

'Because you had to realise that anything is possible if you want it bad enough. Blind faith spurring you on. Just like I want and need you in my life. Doing the jump meant a lot to you, and I wanted to help you succeed.'

'This isn't about the baby, Max. You're the missing part in my world. To think I shut you out and could have lost you makes me crazy. I love you so much. Trust me. It's from the heart.'

She kissed him softly on the cheek, and he revelled in the contact.

Max savoured the gorgeous, feminine smell of her — so exquisite; he'd missed it. He rubbed his nose gently in her hair and kissed her.

'I've waited so long for you to see me properly.'

'I do now. I watched that parachute video. When I saw you falling out of a plane, I realised I couldn't let you fall out of my life.'

Max sloped his warm, ready lips into the curve of hers. It felt like coming home. The home and love he'd craved.

'I had a hunch about your sickness, too. I am a doctor.' He smiled. 'And your mother worries about you. More than you know. We got to chatting about your symptoms. The thought that it could be pregnancy rocked me completely to consider it. But then I figured you'd have told me. Oh, and talking of surprise babies, I've been entrusted to deliver some special news to you in person.'

'News?' Anya quizzed.

'Jenny Murdoch,' Max said with a broad smile. 'She's pregnant too. Early days, and they weren't trying this month. Another happy family,' he said softly. 'When I told you I didn't plan on settling down yet, it was true. But I've struggled since then with the powerful feelings I have for you.'

'And I thought I couldn't risk loving, when the whole time my love for Callum should've shown me just what's possible.'

'Everything is possible. Even our miracle baby.'

'I love you so much. But I don't want you giving up that wonderful job because of the baby,' she told him earnestly.

'I'd only have been hiding myself away in Italy, pining for my bonnie over the ocean.'

She laughed, but his eyes and his voice took on a serious edge to show her how much she meant to him.

'No more bad-boy risk taking, I promise,' he said.

'Maybe sometimes if you're good.' She smiled into his kiss.

Max swept her up into his arms. 'I love you,' he whispered passionately. 'Let me be there for you and your family. We have forever,' he assured her revelling in the bright joy in her eyes. 'Wanting you is my riskiest endeavour, but I'm planning to be a stable and sensible dad and partner from this point on. If you'll have me.'

'I couldn't ask for anything more,' she replied; and, smiling, drew him to kiss her again.

We do hope that you have enjoyed reading this large print book.

Did you know that all of our titles are available for purchase?

We publish a wide range of high quality large print books including:
Romances, Mysteries, Classics
General Fiction
Non Fiction and Westerns

Special interest titles available in large print are:
The Little Oxford Dictionary
Music Book, Song Book
Hymn Book, Service Book

Also available from us courtesy of Oxford University Press:
Young Readers' Dictionary
(large print edition)
Young Readers' Thesaurus
(large print edition)

For further information or a free brochure, please contact us at:
Ulverscroft Large Print Books Ltd.,
The Green, Bradgate Road, Anstey,
Leicester, LE7 7FU, England.
Tel: (00 44) 0116 236 4325
Fax: (00 44) 0116 234 0205

WISHES CAN COME TRUE

Angela Britnell

Meg Harper is shocked when the man she knows as Lucca Raffaele, who stood her up in Italy the previous summer, arrives to stay at her family home in Tennessee — this time calling himself her step-cousin, Jago Merryn . . . Jago is there to acquire a local barbecue business, but discovering the woman who came close to winning his heart is only one of the surprises in store for him. Can they move past their mistrust and seize a second chance for their wishes to come true?

CHRISTMAS TREES AND MISTLETOE

Fay Cunningham

The idea of another family Christmas fills Fran with dread, particularly when she is asked to pick up her mother's latest charity case and bring him along. But Ryan Conway is not what she was expecting. He is looking after his young niece while his sister is in hospital, and Fran decides the pair of them may not be such bad company after all. Then, once the festivities are in full swing, Santa arrives unexpectedly — and Fran's life changes forever . . .

LOVE UNEXPECTED

Sarah Purdue

After being jilted by her fiancé, Nurse Jenny Hale decides to escape the well-meaning but suffocating sympathy of her friends and family by taking her honeymoon alone. On her journey to the Caribbean island of St. Emilie, a crisis throws her together with Doctor Luc Buchannan — who she finds herself falling for. But Luc also carries a heavy burden from his past. Is it possible for the doctor and the nurse to heal each other's hearts?